The
Patrons
Katherine Dempster

Dream Big Publishing
Byron Center, MI

This book is a work of fiction. Any references to historical events, real people, or real locales are used factiously. Other names, characters, places, and incidents are the product of the author's imagination, and any resemblance to actual events or locales or persons, living or dead, is entirely coincidental.

Dream Big Publishing
A publication of Dream Big Publishing
Byron Center MI
Copyright 2016 by Katherine Dempster
All rights reserved, including the right of reproduction in
whole or in part in any form.
Dream Big Publishing is a registered trademark of
Dream Big Publishing.
Manufactured in the United States of America
All rights reserved.
Woman's photo © Kozzi

Summary: Abby Whitmore's world changed forever when her parents tragically died just one month apart when she was only 10 years old. 12 years later her life seemed to be on track and bright when she heads to her small towns pub to celebrate her college graduation with her redheaded spitfire of a best friend, Phoebe Blake. A night that was supposed to be about new beginnings turned into one of unfinished business as soon as she laid her eyes on the gorgeous face of Keiran Bernard. A man that Phoebe not only knew – she despised. Abby quickly finds out that there is an entire world of supernatural beings that live secretly alongside of us and the things that go bump in the night aren't only real, sometimes they're family. And your best friend.

[1. Paranormal – Fiction 2. Romance 3. Fantasy]
978-1523460922
Katherine Dempster
Copyright 2016 by Katherine Dempster
All rights reserved.

Dedication

I want to thank Alicia for being ridiculously inspiring with your talents and for pushing me, Steve for being my favorite cheerleader and ultimate pirate bestie, Jen for being my favorite sounding board and supernatural fangirl sister, Renee for being my first reader and the coolest person I know in Louisiana, and my kick ass husband Greg for having boundless blind faith in anything I do. I know neat people.

# Chapter 1

You can put a white picket fence around anything, but that doesn't make it a home - a home is made with family. Abigail Whitmore's uncle spoke those words to her so many times. She remembered the first time she heard them when she stood on the porch belonging to him and her wonderful aunt Julie - her daddy's younger sister; a fresh new wide eyed orphan at the age of 10. That was 12 years ago this autumn. Her father had passed on after an accidental fall from a roof at a renovation his construction company had just begun work on and, tragically, her mother only a few months later from what she had been told was an extremely rare, extremely aggressive cancer that was diagnosed and fatal all in the same month. That was when Abby was packed up and moved four short blocks over to her new home and what felt like a new life.

Although she was still in the same beautiful little town with the same snowcapped mountains on one end of Main Street and the same dense forest with the same miles of trails on the other end, it would never feel the same to her. It was a close community that swelled with tourists in warm weather to spend holidays on the crystal clear lake on the other side of the woods and welcomed each change of season with festivals filled with food, games and families. But when she looked at it all now, the forest trails were only memories of her mother leading her through the seemingly mile high redwoods, cameras in hand, while she pointed out the different flowers, lush plants and scurrying critters with all the enthusiasm of a curious child. The festivals were heart crushing reminders of her father proudly handing her the toys and prizes he spent a little too much money on to win for his favorite girls. The way he would lift her as if she was light as a feather onto his shoulders before her beautiful mother would wrap her arm around his waist to walk, happy and exhausted, back to their old farm house. Lucy and Adam Whitmore were picture perfect together and loved each other like no else Abby had ever met. Her mother's shimmering blonde hair and skin that always looked sun kissed, even in the darkest days of winter, glowed around the same emerald green eyes that Abby saw every time she looked in the mirror; although her mother always had a sparkle in hers, like a light from within, that Abby never saw in her own. Lucy always found the joy and good unabashedly in everything and could light up the world around her with a blinding smile, seeming to glow as if she were always standing in front of the sun. Her father shared the same dark chocolate hair with his daughter, just as thick and soft, and they had the same pale skin that preferred to burn in the sun. Adam had loved to laugh; he had a deep rumbling laugh that brought crinkles around his deep brown eyes and made anyone who heard him join in. You couldn't help but smile when you were around them; they radiated a love that was contagious. Your heart would be more full just by being near them. And it was an empty hole in Abby's heart that she was always very aware of.

Thomas and Julie Jaimison couldn't have been more welcoming and loving to their only niece, and as it became, their only child. They had such patience for her when she spent her nights either crying until dawn or waking to screaming nightmares and always made sure to keep the memory of her parents alive in stories and pictures set all over the house. They were never able to have a child of their own for reasons they didn't bring up to Abby, but they were very happy to have her as their own. She was close with them before her parents had passed but she grew to love them as second parents quickly. Most people, who hadn't known her before she came to live with her aunt and uncle, would be quick to think Julie was her birth mother because she had the same deep brown hair and fair skin as her older brother and, in turn, her niece. And they strongly encouraged her in everything she did. Whether it was the amazing talent they had to turn a cringe into a beaming smile of pride during her short turn as a thirteen-year-old attempted violinist, the hours they spent scratching their heads at her homework questions, or the miles they drove to every museum they could make it to when Abby decided her dream was to work in one as her career. They never complained at the piles of shoeboxes in her closet of self-proclaimed treasures she had collected and catalogued over the years. And they cheered with her when she was accepted into college for museum studies, never complaining at the hole it left in their savings.

Abby was sitting on the steps of the very porch she stood on when her life changed over a decade ago, now with her graduation cap in her hand – a well-earned new possession for her four years of hard work and the daily commute to the college about an hour away (in good traffic) from her tiny town. How proud her parents would have been to see her today. She could see her mother's radiant face as she stood and clapped for her little girl, her father pulling her in for the warmest of hugs after she collected her diploma. She knew her parents were looking down on her from wherever they were but she smiled to herself at Thomas and Julie's reaction to her big moment today. Her aunt was bawling in joy as she wiped her nose with the tissues she'd hidden in her sleeve, her beautiful face swollen and red from her emotions. Thomas had his arm around her, trying to calm her down, his face tight trying not to laugh at his heartwarmingly enthusiastic wife. He had pulled Abby aside earlier to share how proud he was of her; how proud he was of all she had accomplished. Thomas always made sure the people he cared about knew how he felt but he was not a man that would unabashedly show affection in public. He was a study in opposites with how her parents had been and how his wife was daily, but there was no question that he was a loving man.

"You ok, Abby?" Uncle Thomas pulled her from her thoughts, walking across the porch to sit on the steps beside her.

"Ya, of course. Just enjoying the sunshine." He took the cap from her hands and plopped it on her head.

"You made us very proud today, you know." Thomas smiled as he sat down beside her, bumping her shoulder with his.

"Thanks Uncle Thomas. I'm glad you guys could be there." She meant it more than she could ever say.

"Were you nervous? You didn't look it at all. You walked across that stage like you owned it."

"Nah, I just pictured everyone in their underwear like Aunt Julie suggested. I was too busy thinking about how pervy I felt and trying not to trip to worry about anything else." He laughed as he pulled her under his arm for a hug. "Thanks for being there for me."

"We wouldn't have missed it for the world. You're going to do great things Abby Whitmore and I'm just happy that I to get the honor to watch. Just like everyone who loves you that's watching with pride." He stared off at the road when he said it, the melancholy in his voice told her he meant her parents. He was related to them by marriage but Adam and Thomas had been like brothers. The few memories she had of them were easy to see in all of the photo albums scattered through their house. "So what's the big plans tonight for our fancy pants museum curator?" the smile returning to his voice.

"Hardly a curator." Abby laughed. "Yet." She smiled at the thought. She would be happy to just find a paying job at a museum, let alone curating an exhibit. The idea of moving to the city and away from her little town was a daunting thought for her, though. The Natural History Museum had been her solace while she tried to find her way in the new life that she'd been dropped into and it was her favorite of all of the museums she's spent time in. Thomas and Julie were always so kind to take her a few times a month, before she was old enough to drive herself. Wandering around the cavernous hallways of exhibits transported her to different worlds, strange moments in time that left her wondering where she would have fit in amongst them. The plan was to spend the rest of her life in those worlds, preserving and exploring them. But a small part of her wished that there was a museum of that caliber closer to home. The Daniel Strauss Museum of Tiled Glass on Main Street was pretty but not exactly what she had gone to school for. She'd resigned herself to the fact that if she wanted to find a bigger world she'd have to be willing to go out and find it. No matter how much that scared her.

"Oh, here comes trouble." Uncle Thomas chuckled as he stood up, looking towards the road.

"Oh Mr. Jaimison, I've never." Abby's best friend Phoebe Blake strutted up the walkway; feigning horror at Thomas, she tossed her bouncy auburn hair over her tiny shoulder. "Although a girl could start some trouble in this town. Doesn't mean she should, but she could." A saucy wink sealed her words that made Uncle Thomas shake his head.

"Yes you could, Phoebe, yes you could." He patted his niece on the shoulder. "Let us know if you're heading out for the night, Sunshine." The screen door snapped behind him and Phoebe took his place on the steps.

Phoebe's energy rolled off her in waves, she was a force to be reckoned with and had a voice to match. Abby had heard her before she set eyes on her when she came into her life in the eighth grade and they had become the very best of friends. She had shut down so much with the few friends she had in the few years after her parent's death and Phoebe was just the thing she needed to help her allow herself to be happy again. Mainly because Phoebe had a way of demanding people be happy, and she seemed to always get what she wanted.

"What's up, buttercup? You looked amazing today. I'm glad we went with the blue dress."

"We?" It would be laughable to think Abby had put any thought into the wardrobe choices for the day, or any big fashion moments of her life for that matter. The Fabulous Miss Phoebe was always on pointe when it came to that. From Abby's first disastrous date with her ninth grade crush to Prom and today, she'd always made her friend look her best. Such detail to how one looks could seem shallow and vapid, but Phoebe had a way of making it about a positive attitude, about looking the way you want to feel. She was barely five feet tall, with delicate features aside from her huge green eyes that spoke even more than her booming voice. Her fiery hair fell halfway down her back in bouncy curls that were the envy of many, as was her toned figure that had never seen the inside of a gym. She was dressed in a tight jade dress that was shorter than it should be but she looked amazing as only she could.

"Anyways" she rolled her eyes, "are you ready for fun tonight? I'm taking you to the pub, drinks are on me and if you say no I'll pinch you." She made little pinches towards Abby's arm, her version of warfare since they were kids.

"I can't say no to you buying, so save the pinches. Let me throw on some jeans and we can go."

She jumped up to head upstairs to change into something a little more comfortable for a pub night.

"Oh hell's no!" Phoebe grabbed her arm and stopped her before she could stand all the way up and she awkwardly sat back down, laughing. "You're full on boy bait in that dress and I'm not letting it go to waste!"

"Are you serious?" Of course she was serious.

"Of course I'm serious! Go change if you want but we look amazing. It would be a shame to waste it on an afternoon of sitting on folding chairs listening to boring speeches. Although, Mason did seemed to enjoy the view. Maybe not a waste then." She flashed her saucy crooked smile up at her. "Maybe he's going to be there and would like to see you in that dress again." Mason was in her fourth year Humanities course and was quite a bit to look at but not so much to talk to. She had no idea how he had made it to fourth year in any course when their college wasn't strong on padded sports scholarships. Phoebe had a good heart in wanting Abby to be with someone, but was not of the same mind when it came to finding someone to spend time with. She enjoyed pretty things, including pretty men. Not that she was a completely superficial person, she had a heart that she wore on her sleeve when she cared, but she did seem to treat men as passing fancies that were there for her amusement. She didn't seem to keep any around for long but she did loved to have them around. Abby had never really had strong feeling towards a guy before. She had boyfriends that she cared for but the novelty that Phoebe found in men wasn't for her. Spending an evening having an awkward dinner followed by a terrible movie with a stranger just didn't have the same thrill for her. She had wondered before if romance wasn't for her, and the idea didn't seem terrible. She didn't need to force companionship when she content with what she had already.

"Phoebes no. I told you I don't feel that way about him."

"That's not what the frothy look of lust you have whenever you're around him says, you little tart!"

"Screw you Pheebs!" Abby laughed and pretended to punch her arm when she made kissy faces at her. "It's hardly *frothy* lust." She had wondered what he looked like under his t-shirt, true, but nothing frothy.

"Mm hmm, keep telling yourself that." She twirled her hair in her fingers raising her face up to feel the sun, a pleased smile on her lips.

"I can appreciate a hot guy without wanting to run away to Vegas and elope with him." She stood up and jammed her hands on her hips to steel her point.

"Good lord Abby, that is definitely *not* what you do in Vegas with a man that looks like that! Oh my god I just rolled by eyes so hard I saw the back of my head." she laughed and grabbed Abby's hand to pull herself up. "Now go change and tell those nice old folks not to wait up for us."

"I'm telling them you called them old!" She stuck her tongue out at her as she walked across the porch and went inside. She started to head upstairs to change but her reflection in the hall mirror caught her attention. Phoebe did make a good point about wasting the outfit. She had spent an hour going through Abby's closet the night before when she found this stuck behind everything at the very back with the tags still on. It had been sitting there for six months after it caught her eye in a little dress shop off of Main Street and became the first real impulse buy she indulged in - with the small savings that had been left to her when her parents passed - and the complete opposite of everything else in her wardrobe. She just had a feeling when she saw it that it was going to be perfect for something and she supposed today was just that. It was a gorgeous deep blue and cut just above her knee with a little flare. It fit her as if it had been tailored for her alone, right up to the little capped sleeves and a Florentine neckline that was perfect for the delicate silver heart locket lined with tiny pictures of her parents that Aunt Julie had given her for a graduation gift. Phoebe had spent an hour setting her thick brown hair into big bouncy curls pinned up on one side. It was a very femme fatale from the '40's look and Abby had to smile back at her reflection. For someone who lived in jeans and t-shirts it was fun to look so damn good.

"Aunt Julie?" Abby called out as she turned to make her way down the family photo laced hallway to the kitchen. Her aunt took great care in making their house a home.

"In here, sweetheart" Her cheerful voice called out as she rounded the corner. She looked up from her pile of soapy dishes in the island sink and smiled. "You look so beautiful, Abby. You have a glow like your mother today." Her eyes seemed to drift off in the same way Thomas' had; they both had been as lost in nostalgia as Abby in the past few days. Taking off her rubber gloves she crossed the kitchen to pull her niece into her arms. She was as close as a sister to Lucy Whitmore and they were as thick as thieves. Abby had so many memories of sitting in the back of her mom's car with her mother and aunt chatting away like the best of friends, laughing away at stories she was far too young to understand. Julie stepped back with her hands on Abby's shoulders. "We are so proud of you, you know."

"I know, I know." She felt embarrassed by all the praise and attention today. "Thank you Aunt Julie." Kissing her cheek, she pulled her in for another hug. Julie put her warm hands on Abby's cheeks, emotions of happiness, pride and sadness all swirling together before she walked back to the half washed dishes.

"Are you guys still wanting to go have a look at that apartment tomorrow?" She made a pouty face and crossed her arms, leaning against the island, obviously trying to lighten the mood. Although, the topic of her niece moving out of their home was a pretty sore subject. "You know you're welcome to stay here for as long as you want, sweetheart."

"I know and I'm very grateful, but if I have any hope in getting a placement at the museum I need to be in the city. I can't do the commute anymore, and my car certainly wouldn't last if I did. And honestly, Phoebe's gonna explode if she doesn't have the action of the big city ASAP."

"I know. I hear you. I won't try the guilt trip anymore. Much." She winked at her as she moved back around to the sink to put her rubber gloves on again.

"I'm heading out with Phoebe now. We're going for celebration drinks at the pub." Abby crossed the kitchen to scoop up some of the bubbles from the sink and dot some on her smiling aunt's nose.

"Ok, sweetheart. Sounds like fun." She reached out to take the tiny necklace charm in her hand and smiled. "Call if you want us to come pick you up. It could be a chilly walk home tonight."

"Will do. Thanks." She grinned at her before turning to leave. She was truly grateful to have them in her life - they were two of the most loving people in the world. She grabbed her purse from the coat rack by the front door, slid on a pair of black ballet flats and stepped out into the fresh air that was cooling from the setting sun.

"Yay! You didn't change!" Phoebe clapped her hands and jumped up and down as she made her way down the steps and along the flower lined walkway that led out to the sidewalk in front of the house.

"It seems a waste to only wear it under my grad gown. And I'd hate for you to look so ridiculous all dressed up on your own." Phoebe rolled her eyes at the thought of looking less than put together and laughing they linked arms to set out for the walk downtown to the pub.

Cleary's was the most popular hot spot in town if you had to declare a hot spot in a town of around 1000 people. It had decent food, cheap drinks and was the closest they had to nightlife other than the movie theatre - that had one screen showing movies that no one would call current in the age of online rentals. The bell rang above the door when the girls walked in, the smell of deep fried food pulling them into their usual booth. A quick glance around told Abby that Mason wasn't there yet and she was surprised that she found herself a tiny bit pouty about that. She was feeling pretty confident done up from graduation and could use a night of harmless flirting. God knows that would make Phoebe happy. She'd been spending a lot of time trying to fix her up with guys lately, not that Abby objected, but she's rather spend her time without the awkward small talk. Either way, her eyes did a second crawl around the pub.

"Easy lusty, he's coming around 8. You have a little over an hour until you can jump him."

Abby's jaw dropped in faux disgust, making Phoebe laugh. It was true Mason was gorgeous; tall with broad shoulders, blonde curls that skimmed his ears and bright hazel eyes that did seem to twinkle a little more when he saw her. She just wished she could find any form of intelligent life in them. He was very sweet but not the sharpest pencil in the pack and conversation was pretty tedious at times.

"Jumping him, as you so eloquently word it, is more your M.O. than mine, is it not?" Abby flicked an eyebrow up at her friend and picked up the drink menu from the table.

"Hell yeah it is! I'm not ashamed of it! I love me some men, baby!" The girls cracked up as Phoebe threw her hands in the air in celebration of her anti-celibate stance. "I just want you to come to the dark side, my virginal friend." She reached across the table to pat Abby's hand.

"Virginal? I'm hardly virginal!"

"Abby you know I don't count Glen. For God's sake his name was Glen!" She put her hand to her chest as if the thought might kill her.

"You're such a dick, Phoebe." But she laughed as she said it.

"No, Glen was a dick. Glen was a dick named *Glen*. Ugh." She scrunched her face up in disgust.

There was nothing wrong with Glen's name but she was right, he was a dick. Abby had dated him for a while freshman year in college and, after sleeping with him, found out he was big fan of sleeping with other girls as well. She had found out after he tried to get a piece of Phoebe at a party on campus, while Abby was in the restroom. A swift knee was directed at what Phoebe thought he was and it was over. Her heart wasn't broken over him, but she was definitely hurt when she heard how many girls he'd been fooling around with behind her back. She was sure that she had always had terrible taste in men. Something Phoebe had made her agenda to fix. And Mason was her current answer.

"Hey ladies, looking good today!" David, the bartender at Cleary's, wiped the table down with an old rag, his smoldering smile aimed directly at Phoebe.

"We must be looking good to get you out from behind that bar and giving us the VIP treatment." Phoebe leaned forward across the table with a flirty smile. David was her other agenda – one specifically for her.

"I'd say it's only because it's slow but you would see right through that wouldn't you?" he winked at her and pulled out a pad of paper and pen from his back pocket. Phoebe beamed at his attention.

"Ya, I'd say I would. Better be careful or we'll expect table service every time." Not that she didn't have him dropping whatever he was doing to be the one to serve her every time she was there anyways.

"Anything for you, darling." He gave her a cheeky smile and a wink. "What can I get you? It's grad night, is it not? I assume you're celebrating?" Abby smiled at how smitten he was with her. No one else was in his universe when he spoke to her.

"Nachos, 2 pints and 2 shots of your cheapest whiskey." She smiled sweetly and batted her eyelashes up at him.

"So the usual?" David laughed as he put the paper and pen back in his pocket. "Why do I bother to ask?"

"Well I'm nothing if not consistent." Phoebe purred.

David blew out a breath and shook his head with grin. "Miss. Phoebe you will be the death of me." He turned and headed back to the bar. The girls almost always ordered nachos and beer when they came to Cleary's but the shots were saved for special occasions or celebrations. It was their own little ritual that they held dear. They had a few friends that could be called acquaintances but they were really only close to each other and family. And even then, Phoebe didn't speak of hers to Abby. She never spoke of her parents - Abby had learned years ago to stop asking about them - and had only introduced the grandmother she lived with in passing, even after all the years of friendship that was practically akin to sisterhood. Her family was a non-topic for her, at all times, and Abby had accepted that. Her own mother had rarely even mentioned her family or her past — and would change the subject when she would bring it up — so it wasn't that strange to her. Families, she'd found, were anchors deep in the seabed — strength against the tide for some and a drowning force for others. Phoebe never shared *why* she didn't care to speak about her family but it was the only thing that would make her sad and that broke Abby's heart to see. The same way that she hated to see her mother darken on the rare occasion her family came up. She'd learned that sometimes people shift away from the family that blood gives them to find the family that fits your heart, and that's no one's business but their own. There was a light in Phoebe when she was happy that dimmed when anything about her family came up. That inner light was currently bursting from her as she watched David's tight jean covered butt make its way back to the bar to fetch their drinks.

"Easy lusty." Abby laughed, throwing Phoebe's own words back at her.

She made a pained face. "It's just not fair how good that ass looks in those jeans." Turning back to her friend with a sigh, she pressed her face into a comical frown.

"When are you going to stop playing the role of flirty sorority girl and finally ask him out? Any other guy would be texting you "Why aren't you texting me back?" by now." Phoebe chewed on her lip and avoided Abby's gaze that slowly became a wide-eyed stare. "Holy crap, you really like him don't you? You actually have feelings for him!"

She glanced up and quickly to David who was smiling at her from the bar. Her eyes seemed to have a shadow pass over them before the twinkle returned and she smiled with a grimace. "I think I do. What's happened to me?"

"Tell him. What's stopping you?"

David crossed the pub and put the drinks on the table, tossing another wink at Phoebe before he turned on his heel back to the bar. Phoebe picked up her shot of whiskey and raised it. Abby mirrored her, smiling back, in awe that the uncatchable Miss. Phoebe seemed to have been caught.

"All in good time, buttercup. All in good time." They clinked their cups and downed the amber burn of cheap whiskey before gulping swigs from the beers.

The bell jangled behind Abby signaling the arrival of more customers and Phoebe's head jumped up to see the door.

"That's got to be Mason!" Her voice was a squeal but her smile sank as her eyes flashed quickly at the door and then back to her glass. "Nope not him, never mind." She blew a quick breath before smoothing her hand over hair, plastering a smile on her face. "He should be here soon though. Where's our nachos?"

"What's wrong, Pheebs? Are you ok?"

Phoebe raised her eyebrows "Hmm? What, me? Ya, of course. I'm starving though."

Abby turned around to the door to see what could have startled her friend so much but whoever had come in had blended into the growing crowd of locals filling the small space of the bar.

"Why are you so jumpy tonight? You don't have something planned do you? Oh my god, you didn't say anything to Mason did you?"

Phoebe finished three quarters her beer in a big gulp before covering her mouth in vain to shield a huge burp.

"Oops. 'Scuse me!" She picked up her napkin, dramatically dabbed the corners of her mouth. "I promise I said nothing to Masey-boy other than how hot you look tonight and that we'd be here."

Abby frowned with suspicion at her, trying to decide if she believed her or if she should be bracing for an embarrassing night. It wouldn't be the first time her friend had tried to force a relationship on her.

"I'm going to get a drink at the bar. Maybe slip my number to David finally." She grabbed her purse and waggled her eyebrows as she stood up from the booth. "You want another beer?"

"No I'm good, thanks." She raised her still full beer. For being fairly small people, and not ones who drank often, they could both hold a surprising amount of alcohol. But seeing as how Abby didn't eat much during the day thanks to her nerves about the Graduation ceremony, she was keen to eat something before really imbibing.

"Suit yourself. I'll ask about our nachos too. I'll be right back. Wish me luck!" She turned to march over to the bar, swinging her hips with all her saucy might. Abby laughed at the sight of her and picked up her phone from the table just as it buzzed. It was Mason:

*Hey Abb u guys at Cleerys?*

Smiling down at the screen, she replied.

*Yup just ordered drinks and nachos. Are you guys coming down?*

It buzzed again a few seconds later.

*Ya were just havin beers at marks first see u soon*

Abby's mind perused the idea of taking Phoebes advice and striking something up with him tonight. He was a nice guy after all and sexy as hell.

*Sounds good*

She fiddled with the phone before setting it down, taking a sip from her glass and thinking of all the ways this could turn into an interesting evening. Looking around the pub that had filled quickly with revelers looking to fill their Saturday evening, she glanced over to the bar to check on Phoebe's progress. David was standing at the end of the bar wiping glasses, laughing at something a guy across the bar had said to him. Scanning the crowd for Phoebe she spotted her standing by the hallway to the restrooms, talking to someone with his back towards their booth. He was tall with thick chestnut hair that was mussed on top, clipped short around his ears, and dressed in jeans and a black t-shirt that did little to hide the lean muscles that were apparent even from the distance. Abby took a gulp from her glass, narrowing her eyes when she saw Phoebes' face. Whatever they were talking about wasn't making her happy. Her arms crossed against her, she was speaking in what looked like a hushed anger and when her eyes flicked to her they were filled with fire.

Abby mouthed to her "Are you ok?"

Her eyes calmed a bit and she nodded back, holding her hands up to say stay over there. The stranger's back straightened when she spoke something in his ear before she stomped away. Abby watched him over her glass as he walked down the hallway, out of sight, before turning her eyes back to Phoebe who was making her way to the bar. Her mood switched quickly from angry to lively as soon as David strolled over to her, scratching his slight beard scruff, with a huge grin stretched across his face. They chatted as he pulled her beer and Abby cheered in her head when she saw her *finally* slip him her number. Phoebe tucked her little notebook back in her purse before she picked up her glass and gleamed a smile at him. He watched her walk back over to the table, his dark brown eyes locked on her with a smile that stretched across his olive skinned face until a customer at the other end of the bar whistled for his attention. He rubbed his hands through his short black hair before tearing his eyes from her. He tossed a bar towel over his shoulder and turned to the thirsty man.

Tossing her purse onto the table she slid onto the booth seat. "This outfit just paid for itself! I did it! I finally did it!" She was glowing with the rush of excitement that filled her.

"That's awesome Pheebs! Good for you." She beamed back before stealing a flirty peek at David. He was smiling back at her again. "It's so strange to see you so smitten though! He must be something special, huh?"

"You're damn right he is."

"Who was that guy you were talking to by the hall? You looked pretty pissed."

She looked from Abby to her glass before squishing her face into a grimace. "Ugh, some guy I used to know. He's nobody." She waved her hand dismissing the topic. "David said it's about time when I gave him my number. He could have just given me his I suppose. It's unfair to nature how gorgeous he is."

"What's up, Phoebe? Don't change the subject." Abby didn't like how she was acting so strangely tonight. Red head or not, she wasn't normally that hot and cold with her anger. "What's going on with you tonight?"

"Nothing is going on with me. Don't be so dramatic. He's no one. Honestly! He's just a guy I used to know and I was letting him know that I didn't want to talk to him tonight. No big deal. No drama. I saw you texting - was it Mason?"

Her phone buzzed again just as she asked. "Yes it was and speak of the devil."

*Hey Abb were staying in at marks tonite come over if you want k?*

"They're not coming tonight. They invited us over to Mark's" Abby rolled her eyes at the phone.

"Ew that stoner's house is gross. No way. We graduated college today!" Abby laughed at how Phoebe scrunched her face up at the thought of spending their celebratory night in a pizza box strewn apartment that smelled like weed and stale beer.

She texted him a *thanks maybe next time* message and slid the phone over for Phoebe to read.

"He's the one smitten with you, he should come to you. Girl's night it is then!" She tossed back the rest of her first beer and slid the fresh one in front of herself, smiling. Digging around in her purse she pulled out her compact and lip-gloss, not so subtly turning the mirror so she could see the bar as she re-applied.

"Hardly a girls night when you're going to be making gaga eyes at your meat over there."

Laughing again, Abby looked over at David and saw the guy that was fighting with Phoebe was leaning against the bar now. He was the most gorgeous man she'd ever laid eyes on. He was perched on a stool, his long legs crossed at the ankles; his soft black t-shirt barely contained his arms that were crossed against himself. His tanned skin made his deep blue eyes pop intensely and they were focused right on her. When their eyes locked it felt as if someone had taken the air from the room around her. Her pulse quickened with her breath and she could only pull her eyes away, back to Phoebe, when she heard her mutter under her breath: "Shit."

"Who is that Phoebe? Seriously, who is he?" She wiped her sweaty palms on her lap, willing herself not to look back up at him. She was jarred by the reaction she had to him. She'd never been a girl to swoon, but just looking at that man across the room filled her with thoughts that would have shocked even Phoebe, she was sure. She stared, wide eyed at her. "Phoebe, who the hell is that?"

"My worst nightmare, that's who." Phoebe put her head in hands before looking up at him walking towards them. Abby's eyes flicked between him, the table and Abby's unimpressed face. When he came to stand beside the booth his eyes were still on her. She looked back and forth between them until he said "Hello again, Phoebe. Mind if I join you?" His deep voice sent shivers up and down her spine as he spoke. Abby watched him watching Phoebe with a tight smile on his face. She couldn't imagine what he could have done to enrage her friend so much, or why she'd never heard of him. He clearly wasn't from this tiny town, because there was no way she would have missed that gorgeous face.

"If I said no would you go away?" She looked up defiantly at him with a sarcastic smile, her hands balled into fists on the table.

"No, Phoebe. Not anymore. I'm sorry." The apology was almost a whisper as he sat down beside her. The tension rolling off her suddenly stopped, being replaced by what looked like resignation.

"Fine. Abby, Kieran, Kieran, Abby." She pointed back and forth between them and looked at Abby with a sad crooked smile on her face. She turned towards the bar and signaled around Kieran to David, gesturing for another round of drinks.

"So nice to meet you Abby." His lips twitched in the corners before turning up into a bright white smile. His eyes lit up with a sparkle that seemed to make his face almost glow. It was the most breathtaking grin she'd ever seen and was again taken aback by her reaction to him again. She felt her smile beaming back at him and embarrassment crawled over her when she realized they were so blatantly staring into each other's eyes. Phoebe cleared her throat and Abby pulled her attention back to her friend's unimpressed expression. She picked up her beer and filled her mouth with a gulp to get her voice back.

"Nice to meet you too. How do you two know each other, Kieran?" Her smile returned with a blush when she said his name.

"We were friends when we were really young. Or you could say our parents were friends. Are friends." He turned to her unusually quiet friend as he spoke.

"That's a good way to put it, Kieran. That about sums it up." A gloom was in her eyes when she tried to give Abby a smile. If he had some connection to her parents, Abby could understand her friend's reaction to him. "So we're having a girl's night that you just high-jacked. Next round is on you, fella." She lightly punched his arm, smiling up at him. "I'm just gonna have to make the best of this, aren't I?"

Kieran smiled at her and stretched his arm across her shoulders. "Of course my little devil, I'll buy all night if you let me."

"Watch it Kieran, I don't have to play nice." She had a real threat in her voice that pulled Abby's eyes from him to her. "But it will be what it will be. And here comes my hot piece of ass with some libations to better my mood."

David had three ice cold beers balanced in his hands that reached across the blue-eyed stranger to put right in front of a love struck Phoebe with a wink and an equally smitten smile. A waitress in the short, flippy kilts that were the uniform for the girls a Cleary's came up behind him with the nachos. Her eyes set on Kieran and a flirty smile set on her lips. Bumping David out of the way with her hip, she set the platter right in front of our new friend, leaning forward a little more than she needed to, in a blouse that was buttoned up a little less than it should be.

"Can I get you anything else?" The girls knew the question wasn't for them.

"Thanks, Brooke, I got this." David chimed in. She gave him a glare before turning her kittenish grin back to Kieran.

"You give me a holler if you need *anything*." She walked back to the bar without so much as a glance at the girls or David, who chuckled and rolled his eyes.

"Are you guys good?"

"As good as we'll get, handsome. Thank you." Phoebe's smile became light again when she looked at him. No matter how angry she was, David made her happy again.

"Ok. *Well holler if you need...anything.*" His voice was mockingly high and put a hand on his hip, shaking his butt like Brooke. He laughed and gave Kieran a friendly slap on the shoulder. Laughter trailed behind him as he pranced back to the bar.

Phoebe held up her cocktail, when she could peel her eyes from his butt - again - and presented another toast. "To love, to happiness and to hoping we all can have both."

## Chapter 2

His eyes were as radiant as immense sapphires and they wouldn't look away from Abby. She found it odd to her that she didn't want him to look anywhere else. She had always hated being stared at, especially after her parents died. The hushed whispers between the ones that couldn't bring themselves to actually speak to her about her loss swirled around her everywhere she went, their eyes always on her. A part of her was well aware that she should feel completely creeped out by a perfect stranger looking at her like he was – especially since her best friend seemed to despise him – but she wasn't - at all. And the more he sat across from her, the more at ease she felt with him.

"So how long have you been in town, Kieran?" Phoebe stuffed a nacho chip in her mouth, and stared at the table. "I haven't seen you around in a while. I'd heard you had gone *home*." She over pronounced the last word, having meaning between them that Abby didn't understand.

"I've been around. And now I am *home*." His lips turned up into a smirk, his eyes still locked on Abby. "You have your mother's eyes, you know."

Phoebe choked on her chip, "Kieran, what the fuck?"

"Excuse me?" Abby felt a tug in her stomach. *Who the hell was this guy?* It was one thing to know about Phoebe's parents, but how could he know a thing about hers.

"Stop it, Kieran. I mean it." Phoebe grabbed his wrist and was struggling to keep her voice low. He pulled his hand away from her but turned a very angry glare her way.

"Ok, this is weird. What's going on?" Abby shifted uncomfortably in her seat, her hands wrapped tightly on her glass. Phoebe and Kieran were locked in an unspoken argument, their eyes saying things that their tight mouths weren't. The chill between them was almost palpable.

"Phoebe, answer me. What exactly is going on here? Kieran, did you know my mom?"

His eyes shot back to her for a moment before turning again to Phoebe who scratched a spot on the top of her auburn head with her tiny, manicured finger, her eyes avoiding both of them. She picked up her glass, swigging down the last gulp, before slamming it down on the table. "Well, I guess that's that." She looked to her bewildered friend and shook her head before her eyes set back on Kieran. She slowly drew a breath through her freckled nose, exhaling it in a sigh.

"You can't undo any of this big guy, I hope you know that!" Her lips pursed to stop herself from yelling at him. "But not here. Go pay our bill and we'll all go talk."

Kieran smiled a mile wide and jumped up from the booth, almost running to the bar. Phoebe was staring at the table, slowly shaking her head.

"If this is some kind of graduation prank, you win. You can stop now, Pheebs." Abby was starting to wish she had gone over to the guys rank apartment now. The evening had turned too strange, too quickly.

Phoebe rubbed her face and picked up her purse. "Let's go buttercup, this is a long time coming, I suppose." She reached for Abby's hand when she stood up but her eyes were on David. She'd always been one for pranks, but this is the most dedicated she had ever been to one.

"Whatever you're planning, I'm on to you. You had me going, weirdo. Now sit down, tell me who this guy is and then go back over to your precious bartender." Abby tugged on her hand and she tugged back, lifting her to her feet. Her already pale skin, if it were even possible, seemed blanched.

"Grab your purse. Let's go." She tucked her own purse under her arm, smoothed her fiery red hair behind her ear and stuck out a curled arm for her now overly cautious friend to take. Her tiny lips pursed into a forced smile when Abby looped her arm in hers. "Of all the days to put you in this dress. You look too damn hot for my own good."

Kieran was standing by the door that he held open for the girls. His messy hair tangled in his fingers when he ran his hand through and he backed up against the door, towering above them, giving them room to walk through. The air was cool for a June evening and Abby was glad she'd shoved a sweater in her bag earlier, shrugging the old, worn cardigan on.

"Hang on." Phoebe had stopped just outside the exit. "Wait right here for a minute. And zip it, Kieran. I mean it. Abby – don't move a muscle." She spun on her heel and went back into Cleary's. Kieran was smiling at Abby, looking uncomfortable with his hands clasped behind him. She pressed an equally uncomfortable smile on her face and nodded awkwardly at him, hoping whatever strange joke her friend was playing on her would be over soon so she could slap her silly.

"So how *do* you know Phoebe?" She leaned against the bricked wall of the pub, digging around in her bag for her phone. The door jangled open before he could answer and Phoebe stomped out with a bottle of wine in her hand.

"How did you get a bottle to go?" Abby laughed as she watched her pull the protruding cork out with her teeth.

"I kissed a bartender. Come on then." She took a swig from the bottle and marched down the sidewalk. Kieran and Abby looked at each other, her face puzzled and his laughing. He was very happy with whatever they were up to, but Abby could think of million other things she'd rather be doing. To be fair to herself she admitted some of those things involved her new acquaintance anyways.

"You heard the lady." He gestured for her to follow Phoebe. His long strides quickly catching up to her, Abby quickened her pace to keep up. They walked a short block to the low stonewall that surrounded Willow Park, named such for the monstrous willow trees that swept along a small pond in the center. Wooden benches sat along the walkway that stretched from the wrought iron archway and all around the large pond in the center. No one spoke as they made their way to the bench the girls had declared their own years ago, just up from the water with the largest of the willows rising above it. Phoebe sat down, taking a swig from her bottle before offering it to Abby and patting the wooden seat next to her. She stood uncertainly beside her before sitting but didn't take the bottle. Kieran took a big gulp of the wine, when it was offered to him, seating himself on the bench across from them and setting the bottle on the ground at his feet.

"Oooookay, Pheebs. This is starting to feel a little like the beginning of a movie murder. You've officially creeped me out. You win – can we go now?" Phoebe leaned back on the bench and stared thoughtfully across at Kieran.

"I always knew you'd win, you know. I saw it in her eyes everyday. That something was missing and she was just never going to be happy. And I guess I always knew that something was coming. But I was happy. I am happy dammit!" She bolted up to her feet, making Kieran tense when she grabbed the wine from the ground in front of him and took another big gulp.

"I know. I know you are, but..." he held his hands up as his words trailed off. Abby was frozen watching the bizarre exchange between them. The chill in the air started to move into her bones, and a shiver traced over her that wasn't caused by the temperature. She was getting scared. Phoebe wasn't playing a prank on her, she could tell that now, but she had no idea what was going to happen. Her eyes were the only thing she could move and they darted back to Phoebe when she bellowed to the sky a frustrated yell.

"Well then, where should we start?" Her voice was calm again when she sat down at Abby's side. "Does anyone even know you're here, Kieran?"

"Of, course Gretchen and Erick know."

"Kieran, you know what I mean. Do they know you're *here*?"

"I'd think by now they would, don't you?" Kieran's eyes flickered to Abby for a flash before he looked back at Phoebe, his eyebrows raised expectantly.

"So you have no idea what you're doing? They didn't tell you what you could or could not say? This is just great. Fan-freaking-tastic." She chugged the wine again and then hugged the bottle to her chest.

"Do what? Say what, Phoebe? You're freaking me out. Kieran who the hell are you?" Abby's voice was shaking as much as her body. They were being far too intense now. Phoebe wiped a tear from her cheek.

"I'm so sorry, buttercup. This isn't what I wanted and what we're going to tell you is going to sound ridiculous - especially because we have no idea what we're doing." She glared at Kieran and turned on the bench to face her. When she saw the state Abby was in, her anger melted into concern for her friend. "Oh, buttercup, I'm so sorry. Don't be scared, there's nothing to be scared of. I promise you. Nothing is going to hurt you."

Kieran snorted as he got up and pulled the bottle from her. He kneeled down in front of Abby and offered the wine to her.

"I think you need this more than she does." He moved slowly, trying not to spook her more. She reached for the bottle just as slowly and took a swig. The warmth of the sweet wine drifted down her throat, and his soft voice and crystal eyes calmed her nerves. She started to take deep, slow breaths to steady herself and Phoebe slid over to pull her under her arm, taking the bottle back.

"I'm gonna try to explain this as best as I can, but bare with me ok? Just listen." She leaned her head over to catch her gaze, smiling reassuringly. Abby nodded slightly. Phoebe looked at Kieran, who stayed kneeling beside them, and blew out her own calming breath. "Ok. I've known Kieran since I was little. Since before you and I became friends." Abby's eyes were frozen on her. The light post behind them illuminated her very serious face that was trying to gauge her reaction. Abby nodded again, wanting her to continue. "His parents were friends with my parents," she paused to look at Kieran before turning back to Abby. "And your mom."

Abby was rooted in place. "Your parents never met mine, Phoebe." Her eyes narrowed trying to understand what she was trying to tell her. Phoebe held her hand in front of her.

"Please, just let me talk. This is not going to make sense but I swear on my love for you and our friendship that everything I'm going to tell you is true. I swear I'm not pranking you and I swear I'm not crazy."

Feeling some relief with how earnest she looked, she snatched the wine from her, downing another mouthful of the liquid courage. Phoebe laughed at her and pulled her in tighter under her arm.

"That's a good idea. You might want to hold onto that until I'm done." She leaned her head back, staring at the full sky of stars, trying to find the right words.

"You know that there's an easier way to do this." Kieran's word snapped her head back and her angry eyes landed square on him.

"No Kieran, we *don't* know that. And you know it. Let me try this my way, all right? Unless you'd like to march her right on over Gretchen and Erick's? How happy do you think they are right now?" Her eyes bore into him until he shook his head, looking away to the moonlit pond behind him.

"Ok. You're right. I fucked this up. I get it. But you don't understand what I've been going through do you? And you can't. And I can have Gretchen and Erick remind *you* of that if necessary." His voice was filled with pain that became drowned out in anger as he spoke.

Phoebe looked as if he had slapped her; the anger instantly gone from her face, replaced with a proud indignation.

"Who are Gretchen and Erick? You keep bringing them up. What do they have to do with all of this?" Abby looked back and forth between Kieran who was still glaring at Phoebe, and Phoebe who was now staring off at the water. "Kieran, can you explain this any better?" His attention snapped instantly to Abby when she spoke his name. The anger was gone from his eyes.

"I can do this." Phoebe's looked at him pleadingly. His finger slowly rubbed his chin as he contemplated words that he didn't speak. One nod of his head was all Phoebe needed.

"Our parents all knew each other because they sort of worked together." She gave Kieran a questioning look as she spoke the words. He had humor on his face now and he gave her a shrug of agreement.

"My parents, and Kieran's parents, still do but your mom left." She spoke slowly, choosing each word carefully. "Your mom left when she met your dad. Because he could never be a part of what they did but she couldn't be without him so she gave it up and left."

"Why wouldn't you have told me that before? How is working together such a big secret?" Abby eyed them both, hoping for a clue to whatever they were not saying. "Does this have something to do with why you don't talk about your parents?"

Phoebe jumped up from the bench holding her arms to the sky. "How am I supposed to explain this to her without it sounding like a complete joke?" She looked down at Kieran, pleadingly.

"You could try shrieking at her." His face was pure amusement.

"Fuck off, Kieran. Not helping." Her voice was an angry hiss but somehow seemed to fill the space around us as if she had roared. He laughed at her reaction.

"I don't know then. You said you wanted to do it your way – and I'm trying to respect that - but I'm always on board for my way."

"Ok screw it. There isn't an easy way to say this so I'm just gonna say it. Abby," she paused to steel her face, her hands firmly on her hips "Abby there are things in this world that a lot of people don't believe are real. Supernatural things. But they are. They are all kinds of real and Kieran and I and you and your mom are all a part of it." The words all rushed out at once and she stopped to let her react, biting her lips in to stop the flow of information. Abby's face was blank as she looked between the two. Her brow slowly furrowed as she kept trying to form the right response before she doubled over laughing.

"Supernaturals?" She barely got the word out between laughs, her breath catching. "We're all *supernaturals*?" A fit of laughter stopped any other response. She took a swig of the almost empty wine bottle when the cackling subsided. "Your whole stupid prank was to try and trick me into thinking we're werewolves or something? Phoebes, long game for a lame joke."

Phoebe just stared at her, hands still locked on her waist.

Kieran's snicker was the only sound in the park. His face was twisted trying to keep his laughter in as he shifted from his knees to sit on the walkway, his back against the bench beside Abby.

"Can I please step in now Phoebe? She's looking at you like you have two heads. You can't explain it to her like that – she needs to understand it like we do, like *I* do."

"Ok, joke's over. I'm done. Not impressed either, Phoebes, pretty lame. You had me going for a while there, but not a fun prank at all. I'm going home." She grabbed her bag and started up the walkway. This wasn't funny anymore and she was cold, tired, out of wine and in no mood to play along.

"Ok, I give up. Do it." Phoebe's voice was quiet and resigned but loud enough to make Abby stop and turn around.

Her heart felt like it had stopped in slow motion, the air in her lungs slowly drawn out when she turned to find Kieran standing right behind her. His eyes were all she could see when he softly put his hands on her cheeks and leaned towards her, almost nose to nose. She suddenly felt like she was struck by lightning, deep underwater and everything disappeared around her in a fuzzy haze. Swirls of colors around her made her feel like she was falling when her mother's voice filled her head and she slammed to the ground. Even though she couldn't make out anything around her, she knew she wasn't in the park anymore. It was all a blurry swirl around her - like when she had too much to drink and just wanted to plant a foot on the floor to make it stop - but she was sure she could hear her mother speaking. She rubbed at her eyes trying to focus on anything.

"You need to understand how special you are my love." Another woman's voice rang out around her. "You need to understand how important you are to us. There is no future written for you!" Abby was starting to be able to focus on an ornate desk with a woman sitting in a high backed chair behind it. She rubbed her eyes again and squinted at her. Blinking rapidly, she could make out, what appeared to be her mother but much younger than she had ever known her to be.

"I love him, Mother. How could you wish anything more than that for me!"

Abby would know her mother's voice anywhere.

The older woman spoke again and Abby strained to make out the features on her face. "Any mother wants love for her children, but you can't choose one of their kind! It's not for us and it's not for them! You can't give away the immense gift you been given on a youthful whim! Do you know how often we are born without our mates ingrained in us? Take responsibility for what you've been given! You have the opportunity to find love on your own – "

"I have!" Hearing her mother sob was crushing her heart.

"NO! You have found foolish fancy with a pet. I love you Lucy, you know how much I love you. You are my daughter, my heart, and I want you to be happy. But with our privilege comes a great responsibility. All I ask of you is to wait. Don't make any decisions right now that could have devastating results for all of us. You don't know that you're truly in love, you're so young still."

"You, mother do not know what love is. Not like I do. You have no idea what it's like to find the other part of your heart so randomly in the world. How deep you feel that."

"Don't you dare assume I know nothing of love solely because you feel it differently."

Everything started to spin around her again and the foggy vision in front of her twisted away. She was screaming for her mother when the cool air slammed against her face as the pavement slammed against her back. Phoebe dropped in front of her, panicked.

"Abby? Abby! Talk to me. Are you ok?"

She could feel her hands on her face, her eyes searching for signs of life. Abby turned her head just in time to wretch all over the grass.

"Abby, my god, are you ok? What have you done? Kieran, what did you do?"

She pulled herself up and turned to see those magnetic blue eyes gazing down.

"What had to be done" He answered her without taking his eyes from Abby.

She felt herself sinking back into the ground, as tired as when she had to be up cramming for finals for days, the nausea subsiding.

"What the hell was in that wine?" Her eyes closed and she fell into darkness.

Chapter 3

Abby was aware of the pain in her head before she even registered that she was awake. Cheap whiskey was officially off of the menu from now on. She only remembered drinking the one shot but it had to have been much more to feel like this lukewarm death. She rubbed her eyes trying to crush the thumping in her brain, sitting up in bed, wishing she had remembered to close the curtains before falling into bed. Then she realized she didn't remember falling into bed - or coming home. She held her head trying to remember anything - she knew there was no way she had drunk that much. Memories of Cleary's came back with each blinding thump. And then she remembered those bright sapphire eyes.

"Morning buttercup." Phoebe was sitting on the end of the bed, a pained smile on her face. "So… that happened, huh?" she forced a laugh and handed over a bottle of water. Abby could only stare at her, water bottle now in hand, no words forming. Whatever the hell that was that happened the night before felt too real but even more insane. "I'm guessing you have questions?"

Abby rubbed her eyes and then stared at her. "Questions? Are you serious? Yes I have questions!"

"Sweetie, I love you but you don't get to be mad at me, ok?"

"I'm sorry, I don't get to be mad at you? What the hell was all of that? Did you roofie me for the sake of a prank? Did you think that was funny? I don't get to be mad? I'm pissed, Phoebe!" Abby's outburst made her head throb even worst, a blaze of pain igniting behind her eyes.

"I have no clue what I'm doing." Phoebe spoke the words more to herself. "Before I tell you anything, I'm going to do something that will make you'll feel much better, ok? It should take away the pain in your head. Trust me." She leaned forward to take Abby's hands, before she could question the ridiculousness of being asked to trust her, and shut her eyes. Instantly there was a chill that started as a tingle in the top of Abby's head that shivered down her skin, the calm floating through her. The burning pound in her head started to melt away. Her eyes lazily fluttered open "Better?"

"What was that? Can you, please, start to explain yourself and stop adding to the things that are freaking me out?" Abby chugged down half of the bottle of water, the cool relieving the desert that had taken up camp in her mouth.

"You would have liked that during finals, right? Does your head feel better?" she laughed and widened her eyes with an overly friendly grin.

"How did you do that?" The calmness, that followed the lost pain, gave way to the anger her confusion was creating and was far fiercer without the searing in her brain now. "What did you put in that wine? And who the hell is Kieran?" Abby's rage combusted when Phoebe giggled and grinned as if she was having just a mere tantrum, not losing her mind. "Phoebe! I puked in the park! None of this is funny!"

"I'm sorry, I can't imagine how strange this is for you. Although it's pretty weird to me, too." She slid up the bed to sit beside her and slowly reached for her hand again. "I shouldn't laugh but it is honestly strange for me too. I don't have much experience with explaining the world, as I know it, to someone who has no idea of it. And I had convinced myself that I wouldn't have to." Abby let her take her hand but said nothing, her face tight with apprehension. "Ok. Let's give this a go." She rubbed her little thumb over her lips; her eyes crinkled as she stared out the window as if the words she were looking for were in the yard below. "There are…things in this world that…" Frustration was making her words labored. "Ok, straight as an arrow." She ran her hand over her hair and tossed it behind her." You know how we like to watch late night movies that scare the crap out of you and I always laugh at them? I could kind of be in one of those movies. And Kieran. And you." Her face was strained when she weighed the words, trying to decide if she had chosen the right ones. When Abby didn't move, didn't speak, she continued. "They're pretty much as real as you are confused right now. And since you're…since you're…"

"Since I'm what?"

"Different, Abby. Different from what you think you are and what you think everyone is and it's not my place to tell you any of this, which was made very clear to me last night, but I want you to know I'm here for you like I always have been. And how I always will be, buttercup." Her voice was casual and light but her expression seemed resigned, scared, and angry all at once. Phoebe's body all at once stilled, her eyes turning to the picture window that filled the wall beside Abby's bed. "And just like that it's all over. Stay here, buttercup, I'll be right back." Her head was down as she made her way through Abby's bedroom door and disappeared down the hall.

Abby tried to understand what Phoebe was playing at. Her nerves were on high alert with the way she had spoken to her, the strange things that had happened the night before and how she was able to take her headache away just by holding her hands. Phoebe was not a great actress, but there is no way that she could believe in monster movies. Abby threw her quilt off and pulled her tired body from the bed, noticing that she didn't even remember putting on the shorts and tank top she had apparently slept in. Slinging on her fleecy purple robe she peered out the window when she heard the slam of the front door screen. No one was to be seen on the walkway meaning Phoebe hadn't left. *Different, Abby. Different from what you think you are...* The words turned over in her head.

"Hello Abby."

Abby jumped with a start and spun around to find a woman standing in the doorway. She was very small in stature but seemingly very imposing. Her pale blonde hair neatly piled on her head above a beautiful but serious face. Phoebe peeked around her, an uncomfortable grin directed at her startled friend.

"Hello." Abby stepped timidly back from the stranger who was now making her way through the door, her sharp jade eyes scanning the room - eyes that Abby immediately recognized as her mothers and her own. The eyes she saw in the hazy dream the night before that were addressing her mother's younger self - eyes that had now turned to settle on Abby.

"I'm can assume this is difficult for you."

Abby's heart pounded in her chest when she heard the woman speak; the same voice as the dream. She was frozen in place regarding the woman standing in front of her. Her eyes, her lips, the glimmer of gold in her hair – Abby's breath caught in her throat.

"You're my Grandmother." She wasn't asking, she knew. She seemed far too young to be her mother's mother – she looked barely older than she did in the dream, or whatever the hell it was that she saw, but there no question she was her Grandmother. Her face softened for a flash of a moment, closing her eyes her lips twitched, before the stoic mask was back in place when she locked eyes with her again.

"I am." She lightly pulled at the hem of an expensive looking blazer. "You are quite perceptive, my dear. My name is Gretchen." She motioned towards the desk chair by the window. "May I?"

Abby's mouth opened and closed a few times before words could find their way out. "Yes, of course. Please." She, herself, sat on the edge of her bed staring at the woman she had heard nothing of, a woman her mother avoided speaking of at all costs, a woman she had a deranged vision of last night when a gorgeous stranger merely put his hands on her face.

"So, my lovely, that is why I'm here."

"I'm sorry, what?" Her attention turned between her brand spankin' new granny sitting at her desk and her best friend, who was as good as a stranger to her right now, sitting on the edge of her bed, quietly staring at the floor. What exactly were Phoebe and Kieran? And how could just putting their hands on her have such an enormous effect on her. A heat washed her face when she considered that it wasn't such a big surprise that Kieran's hands could.

"Abby, I believe that look on you face means that your thoughts have turned to a certain gentleman we both know. I know that look and it's one of the reasons I am here." She smiled tenderly, "It is not, however, what I am hear to discuss with you now." Her lips pursed and her left eyebrow rose after she spoke. Her eyes sparkled the green that Abby saw in the mirror and in the memories of her mother, but had far more behind them. There was a wisdom that she found intimidating.

"I had always hoped we would meet, although, I had hoped that you would have been introduced to me by my daughter, your mother." Her eyes never left Abby. "You are an exceptional girl in an extraordinary situation." Her eyes flashed to Phoebe. "You have done a wonderful job of protecting her and it will be remembered. However, this was never a choice I supported or accepted." Phoebe's tension was rolling off her in waves, making Abby very uncomfortable. Gretchen's affection was clear when she addressed Abby, but there was terrifying authority in her voice towards the frightened girl beside her.

"I'm sure you have many questions and they will all be answered but we need leave immediately. Things have not advanced in a manner that I would have preferred. It will be for the best to have you at home for now." She stood, smiling again at Abby.

"But I *am* home. Please just tell me what's going on."

"I am well aware how overwhelmed you must be, but it will be explained in due time. I am here to collect you, to bring you back to your rightful place with our family. Your family here will be compensated and made well with what has happened."

"What? Compensated for what exactly?" Confusion and anger were twirling inside, making her voice trill. "I'm not going anywhere until I talk to my Uncle!"

"You will speak to them in due time, I promise you my dear. Anything you say to them right now will only alarm them. They are not as we are, as you are, my dear." She smoothed her jacket again.

"Ma'am, I...." Phoebe started to speak.

"You are no longer being given the lenience to which you have been accustomed to, wailer." Gretchen's words were cold.

Phoebe's eyes returned to the floor. "I'm sorry...." Her words were barely a breath.

"There is no reason to be frightened, my dear. I ask you only to join me at my home to allow me to speak with you. Please be calm. I want nothing more than for you to come of your own free will." She lovingly gazed at her granddaughter, but it wasn't enough to keep her placid.

"My own free will? Are you freaking kidding me, right now?" She sprung from bed, stumbling around to the other side, desperate to put as much distance between them as she could in her small bedroom. "I'm done with all of this. I'm not leaving with a complete stranger and my insane best friend who apparently thinks we're werewolves or witches or something!"

"Werewolves or witches? Oh good lord, Phoebe, what have you said?" Gretchen put a hand to her forehead, obviously exasperated.

"I didn't say we're…"

"Enough! Enough of all of this nonsense - my patience has been wasted." Her eyes blazed brightly as she quickly strode to her granddaughter. "You have left me no choice, Abby."

Abby tried to lean away from her Grandmother when she raised her hands to her alarmed face. The feeling of falling through warm air consumed her again.

Chapter 4

Her bed had never felt so comfortable, and Abby stretched out her arms and legs, appreciating the delight she felt with each pull. She scrubbed her face with the palms of her hands, as she let out a big yawn and opened her eyes, expecting the light of the morning. But it was night, and the moon shone through a window that wasn't hers, onto a room that wasn't either. The room was huge, as was the bed she was in, and was quite ritzy – Pinterest-style fancy – from what she could make out in the dark. Her eyes focused on a large ornately carved wooden door at the opposite end of the room, as it slammed open. Phoebe, dressed in her sweats and her fiery hair twisted into a mess on top of her head, ran across the space between them to jump on the bed. Abby looked down to see she was still in the shorts from earlier but her favorite ratty sweatshirt, that once belonged to her dad, was now covering her tank top.

"I'm so sorry Buttercup! I'm so sorry." She sat beside her but looked at Abby as if she would shatter. "Are you ok?"

"What the hell, Phoebe?" Abby sat up against a mound of goose down pillows.

"I know, I'm sorry." Phoebe's face was concerned but shadowed with, what Abby thought was, anger.

"What the hell keeps happening to me? Where are we?" She pulled the soft covers up against her chest, looking around the posh room.

"This is the Patron's Manor – your Grandparent's house."

"So I'm a prisoner now?" Her voice was rising as quickly as her anger. "You can't keep me here! Thomas and Julie will come looking for me! They'll call the police!"

"You're not a prisoner here, Abby. Calm down, seriously. It's ok, I promise." She slowly raised her hands in front of her, trying to calm her now hysterical friend. "I promise. You're here because showing you all of this is a lot easier than trying to explain it. I felt like I was trying to describe what salt tasted like to someone that has never had it."

"What are you going on about? How in the hot hell did I get here?" Her voice was still angry but deep slow breaths started to calm her. It wouldn't help her to get out of there if she was hyperventilating.

"That would be your Grandmother. She told you that she wanted you to come with her, and what she wants, she gets." Phoebe nervously laughed at the furrowed confusion that took over Abby's face.

"She knocked my out?" It sounded ridiculous to her as soon as she spoke the words. The idea that such a delicate, prim woman would have rough handed her was laughable.

"She didn't hit you or anything. She just has…abilities…that can…" she tried to find the words that fit, "She can make things happen, in your mind." Her face was twisted with frustration. "Does that make any sense to you at all?"

"You're telling me that my Grandmother, who I just met for the very first time by the way, has mind control powers. She can control people's minds like the TV vampires? That's what you're telling me? Seriously?"

Phoebe exploded in giggles. "Vampires? Ya, no they can't do that. They wish."

"Do you hear yourself? Phoebe? Do you hear how ridiculous you sound right now?" Abby leaned forward to Phoebe, making sure she was looking her square in the eye.

"I know exactly how ridiculous I sound - to you. But I think you've been witness to enough weird shit that you could at least hear me out. Let me try to explain."

Abby had to admit to herself that her friend seemed as serious as a heart attack. "Ok…go on." She leaned back against the plush stack of pillows again, her arms wrapped defensively across her.

"It's called carriaging." She said it matter of factly, as if she had said shopping. "It's a tool Patrons use when they need to persuade a mort…a people." She smiled meekly, her fingers twirling and tugging incessantly at her red hair.

"I'm sorry, a people?" Abby shook her head as she laughed. "And you keep saying Patron. Like Patron's manor. My mom's maiden name was Ambrose not Patron. How could her parents have a different last name?"

"Patron isn't a last name. It's who they are. What you are."

"What I am? I'm a Patron? Like of the arts or something? My grandmother is some kind of psychic philanthropist? Is that what you're telling me?" Abby rubbed her forehead, a pain starting to form once again.

Phoebe chuckled to herself as she looked around the room as if it held the secret to how to approach the conversation somehow. "This is really hard. I'm starting to think your Grandmother was right – I should just stay out of it. But I want to be here for you." Phoebe reached for Abby's hand, twisting their fingers together. "I have to find the right words." She gave another thoughtful gaze around the room, took a deep breath and turned back to Abby, whose attention was solely on her. "Remember how I told you supernatural things were out there, that they were real?" Abby nodded and started to speak before a hand was raised in her face to stop her. "No just let me try to explain. No questions yet, ok?" Abby nodded, but pulled her hand back and crossed her arms against herself again. "Well, they are. And The Patron's are a type of supernatural being that are a sort of government? I think that might be the right word. They're in charge of all of the others that live apart from the people like your Aunt and Uncle and your dad."

A knock on the door had Phoebe jumping from the bed and jogging to the door. She opened the door and stepped out of the way for a friendly looking older lady with sweet brown eyes and short white hair curled neatly. Her black dress and white apron were obviously a uniform of some kind. She pushed a cloth covered wheeled cart into the room with an enormous silver covered platter and glasses set on top. Behind her, a man that was no taller than three feet high, and had skin an ashen grey with ears that appeared to be four times larger than average, just like his nose. He carried an ice bucket with a bottle of champagne in little hands that led to long claw-like fingernails. His eyes, that were black as ink, glanced briefly at her before returning to Phoebe where they stayed.

"I know guys, big news but move along." She grabbed the glasses from the tray. "Don't make me speak to Gretchen." They nodded quickly and disappeared back out the door. "Glass of bubbly?" Smiling ear to ear, she grabbed the bottle and launched the cork across the room. Abby's eyes were popped with shock.

"Is it the surprise of cocktails or Barnaby that has you in such a state?" Phoebe giggled, pouring into two flutes and successfully overflowing both – causing more giggling. She handed a glass to Abby who took it from her, her eyes not leaving the door. "Ah, so Barnaby it is. He's a Goblin." She raised her glass, "Cheers!"

Abby snapped her attention back. "Phoebe! That's not very nice! What a mean thing to say!"

"Why? He *is* a Goblin. If anything I've said to you hasn't made you believe, seeing Barnaby has to convince you I'm not pranking you. For god's sake, Abby! You saw him! That's nothing you've ever seen before, but there it is! Evidence that I'm not full of shit!" She downed her flute of champagne in one gulp and leaned over to grab the bottle from the bucket she'd set on the floor beside the bed.

Abby's eyes flashed from the door to Phoebe, who was waving her hands around emphatically, and back. She downed the glass just as quick and narrowed her eyes. Phoebe froze waiting for a reaction.

"A goblin? That was a goblin?" Abby looked at, but beyond, the door. "A goblin named Barnaby just served me room service - at my brand spanking new Grandmother's house. My brand spanking new Grandmother who is some kind of supernatural royalty." She reached her glass out to Phoebe who topped it up from the frosty bottle.

"Royalty! That's closer to what you are. Good word for it, *princess*." She winked and filled her own flute. Abby stared wide-eyed, her jaw at a new level of dropped. "So I should have started with some kind of joke about you being a pseudo-princess right off the bat? You have an inner diva that I never knew about!" Phoebe crawled up to the top off the bed to join her on the pile of pillows.

"Well that bloody goblin sure had some weight." A laugh started deep inside her, in the place that started to believe all of the insane things she's been told and had been shown. It rumbled out of her until she was laughing so hard that Phoebe couldn't help but join in. "This is insane. All of this! This is real isn't it, Pheebs?"

"Afraid so, buttercup." She grinned widely when she clinked their glasses. Abby's laughter quickly turned to tears, overwhelmed with everything that her world had become. She wiped her eyes with her sleeve and dragged her hand under her runny nose.

"Ew! Abby, gross! Go wash your hands!" She feigned gagging but laughed more.

"Ya, ya. Sorry princess." She ran her nose down palm to elbow just to gross her out more.

"Seeing as you're more of a real kinda, sorta, not really actual princess now, you best get your shit together. The bathroom is over there." She pointed to another, smaller ornate door beside the giant window. Abby flipped her off and smiled before heading to the washroom.

She smacked her hand along the wall inside the bathroom until she found the light switch and flicked them all up. The room was flooded with pot lights that lit up a bathroom that belonged in a fancy resort suite. A massive stone shower stood in one corner, so big that there was a door on each side into it. The opposite was the deepest tub she had ever seen placed in front of floor to ceiling windows. When she moved towards them she recognized Lake Constant, a lake that she spent a lot of time swimming in with her parents as a kid. It was a beautiful, expansive lake only twenty minutes from her house. Her thoughts drifted to splashing along the shore with her dad, her mom curled up on a blanket with her books. *Was she able to see this house from the sandy patch where they always set up at, or did she choose to go to that spot because she couldn't see it?* She certainly didn't remember any houses along the lake, let alone any 'Manors'. She wondered if her mother brought her here as a little girl to swim where she did as a child? It made sense now why she was always so quiet when they spent the day there. She had always assumed it was because she was so relaxed, but looking back now, as an adult herself, she could see how there was a sadness about her. She walk from the window to the huge double sinks and turned on the faucet, splashing her face when the water turned warm. Pulling a fluffy towel from the rack she dried her face, already feeling better for it. She eyed her knapsack set on a long wooden counter beside the shower, smiling to herself knowing that the ever-resourceful Phoebe would have made sure she had it. She didn't have to look in to know that she had packed everything she could need. She rooted through for something comfortable and pulled out her favorite duck covered fleece pajamas. Her face cream, hairbrush and a scrunchy were rolled up inside them and her heart warmed with how well her friend knew her. She tugged her day old pajamas off and pulled on the fresh clothes, after briefly considering a hot bubble bath in the tempting tub. She would have fallen asleep instantly in the warm soothing water and there was way too much to talk about, so instead ripped the brush through her hair and twisted it up into the elastic. She opened the door to find Phoebe lying on her stomach on the bed, her hand propping up her head, with a devilish grin splashed across her face. She looked so tiny lounging across the impressive four-poster bed. The deep walnut wood, matching the wide trim and crown molding that circled the room, was carved in delicate swirls of flowers. The silver tray from the trolley was set atop the plush red duvet in front of her; the smells of nachos drifting across the room made Abby's stomach rumble.

"Champagne and nachos. How very Phoebe of you." She shook her head, laughing when Phoebe grabbed a greasy chunk of chips and cheese, shoving the whole mass in her mouth.

"Feel better, buttercup?" The words were barely audible through her chipmunk cheeks. She wiped her mouth with a black fabric napkin and reached over the edge of the tall bed for her crystal flute that she'd set on the floor.

"I do, a little. The shower is so big in there that it has an entrance and an exit door! That's Lake Constant out there isn't it?". She pointed at the enormous window, that she'd failed to look out of earlier.

"It is. Pretty view isn't it? It's not so bad here. I spent so much time avoiding it, I'd forgotten about all the perks." Another handful of chips crammed into her mouth.

"So this is my Grandmother's house?" Abby looked around at the beautiful room they were in. It was the largest bedroom she'd even seen. The furniture alone seemed large compared to the double bed and small writing desk of her cramped room. It was gorgeous but felt more like a hotel than the coziness of her bedroom. She picked up her glass again and sat down on the bed.

"Well it's your Grandmother's and Grandfather's home, yes."

"I have a Grandfather too. Huh. What else does today have in store for me?" She chuckled into her drink.

"You do. Erick, Mr. Ambrose. He's a wonderful guy, honestly - so kind and warm. You'll love him, everyone does."

"Gretchen doesn't seem to like you very much. What's that all about?" Abby crawled back up to the pillows, trying not to spill her glass, feeling the warmth of the drink spreading through her.

"She's got far too much to deal with to care about me." She passed her a plate over flowing with chips and guacamole.

"Why would you have to speak to her about looking at me?" She sunk into the mountain of pillows and took a sip of the sweet, chilled champagne. Phoebe was right - this wasn't all bad.

"What?" She dug around on the plate of food until she found another cheesy mouthful.

"You told Barnaby and that lady that you wouldn't want to have to speak to my grandmother when they were looking at me."

"Oh, them. Well you're a huge curiosity around here with all of us. They've been told not to stare and make you uncomfortable. Your Grandparents want you to be happy here, they really do. But you're as unusual to them as they are to you, so, your Grandparents have spoken to the staff about how they should not make you feel, I don't know, like, odd?"

"They have an actual staff here?" Abby tried to imagine living a life that included staff living in your home.

"A *lot* of staff. This house is huge and your grandparents are a big deal, like an important kinda big deal."

Abby looked around the swank room again, her eyes settling on the expensive bottle of champagne. "So am I rich now?" She smiled at Phoebe when she laughed. "What? Look around us. It's a pretty fair question." Holding up the crystal glass to her, she worked her best posh face.

"Well your family is not hurting for money, that's fair to say. But I've been privy to your ATM receipts and, no, you're not rich." Abby tossed a pillow at her and stuck out her tongue. Phoebe placed the tray back on the trolley and jumped back on the bed with the bottle.

"So are we drinking until it's easy for you to answer questions or until it's easy for me to hear the answers?" Abby held her glass out with her question.

"Buttercup, if you want to talk, by all means we should talk. Because this is how it is now and we can't change that. I just thought you needed a drink after today... and yesterday." She filled the glasses before pressing the bottle back into the ice and rolled over onto her side. "Are you ok? I just realized I haven't asked you if you're ok."

"I'm better than I should be and that's the strange part for me. I should be more freaked out or unbelieving of all of this. Of *all* of this." She waved her hand around at the room. "I'm glad to have you here with me though."

"I'll always be here for you." They clinked their glasses and took a gulp. She knew she meant it too.

She took another sip from the glass as she stood up from the bed to look out the enormous windows. It was a very different view than the bathroom, with a darkened forest as far as she could see lit only by the moon. What could that forest have in it if all the creatures of stories and nightmares are real? What if those creatures were in this very house?

"So what exactly is real? Monsters and goblins, wise." She sat in the picture window, curling her legs up against her body.

"Pretty well any supernatural being you can think of. They're all real in a sense – not like in the books and movies usually, but real."

Abby's mind swirled with the creatures in the Midnight Mania marathons they spent Saturday nights watching. "You mean like vampires and werewolves?"

"Yup."

"So…are you a vampire?" She kicked her legs out, sitting up at attention. "Oh my god - is Kieran a vampire?" If those stories were true, that would explain why he was sexy as hell.

Phoebe cracked up. "No we're not vampires. Kieran's a Patron like you. I'm…something else. There's a reason why all of us are just stories to them – because of your family. They keep regular people from finding out about us being real."

"So let me pull all of this together; Supernatural creatures are real…"

"Creatures? Seriously? Rude." Phoebe's eyes narrowed and pursed her lips before laughing.

"Ok, ok, very funny. Cut me some slack here."

"You're right, I'm sorry." She smiled warmly at Abby. "You're handling all of this really well."

"Thanks, I guess." She leaned back against the window frame, trying to gather her jumbled thoughts to rationalize what had happened in the last 24 hours. "So Vampires are real? Like, actually real?"

"Yup." Phoebe's lips pushed into a tight smile and shrugged her little shoulders.

"And Werewolves?"

Phoebes face scrunched up in thought, weighing the question, before replying "Kinda, ya" and shrugging her shoulders again.

"Zombies?"

Phoebe cracked into a fit of laughter. "Zombies? Oh sweetie, you watch too much TV!"

"Seriously? Are you serious right now? With all I've been told, Zombies are ridiculous to you?" Abby downed the rest of her glass and walked over to crawl up on the bed again.

"Ok, fair enough. You're right. I've never talked to Transients about this before. It's weird."

"What do you mean by transients?" Phoebe's turned red at Abby's question and she picked a fluff on the bed.

"That's what your dad was. And your Aunt and Uncle." She avoided her eyes, making Abby push further.

"That doesn't answer my question, Phoebe." She tilted her head down to get her attention. "Why do you call them that?"

"Because they don't last here as long as us."

"Are you telling me you're immortal?" This was turning back into a Midnight Madness movie and fast.

"No, not at all! I'm not immortal. We just live a lot longer than they do. We age slower I guess. There are some that are but most of them you don't want to mess with. You don't even want to talk about them."

"So am I...that? A transient?"

Phoebe sighed, turning to face Abby. She chewed her lip while she thought about the question. "I don't know. I mean you are because your dad was, but your mom was a Patron so you're a Patron by birthright. I just don't know how much of what makes a Patron you have. Or you are. I honestly don't know, none of us do. I'm sure your Grandparents have a better idea but it's not like they would tell us. That's why you're such a celebrity around here. None of us have ever known a Patron that fell in love with – and started a family with – a transient. It's just not done!"

Abby tried to process the idea of her mom being something other than what she had always known her to be. Let alone Supernatural.

"How did I get here? Why do I keep waking up in beds with no memory of how I got there?" It was creepy thinking of her unconscious body being dragged around town.

"I tried to tell you about it back at your house. Carriaging. It's a way of taking away memories or planting new ones. Or shutting down thoughts and awareness completely. Patron's are the only ones that can do it and only to transients. Except what Kieran tried to do to you last night. That's a Patron thing that I don't really get but I told him that you're only Patron on your mother's side so we had no idea what it would do to you. That's why the moron made you sick." Remembering the nearness of him made Abby smile until she remembered the puking and the headache when she woke up in her bed, no memories of how she even got into the house.

"Do Aunt Julie and Uncle Thomas know anything about this?" It seemed impossible that they could keep something so spectacularly insane from her.

"No they know nothing. They couldn't. Like I said, the Patrons keep all of this from anyone who isn't a part of our world. It would be a disaster."

"So I'm the only one that isn't completely a part of all this that knows about this?" The idea frightened her. If she were the only one like her; she was some kind of freak. She couldn't imagine many people - *are they still called people?* - she couldn't imagine they would be keen to want her around.

"Oh no, not at all. The lady that came in earlier - Maggie - she's a transient. There are a few people here that are. They're our Familiars."

"Ok, now what does that mean? Familiars?"

"They're Transients that have been trusted with knowing about all of this. They help with things that need to be done. Some are Empaths as well – people who are transient here, but are touched with our energies. They can sense us, and some can use that power. I guess that's what you'd call a witch." She poured the last bit of champagne into Abby's glass.

"Witches? Like cauldrons and brooms?"

Phoebe chuckled. "Ya, that idea but without the flying broomstick. They use energies kind of like how I did earlier to make you feel better."

"So what are you then? Do you have any other magical powers?" Abby got excited at the idea her best friend could do magical things – and wondered if there was anything enchanted she herself could do.

"I'm your best friend. That's all you need to know for now." She stood up and dropped the bottle upside down into the bucket. "We're out of drinks, and I'm really tired. Can we talk more tomorrow? I really just want to go to bed and you definitely need to get some sleep. You have a lot more to deal with tomorrow." She pulled Abby in for a quick hug and turned for the door. "We'll talk more after we both have a good night sleep. Your Grandmother is going to explain a lot of the things I can't tomorrow, I promise."

"Am I going to be allowed to go home soon?"

"You can't just go back home to pretend everything is back to normal, Abby. You need to talk to your Grandmother before you go anywhere."

"So I *am* a prisoner then, aren't I?" Abby's sense of calm about the situation was slipping away.

"It's not like that, I swear to you. You're perfectly safe here and you can leave at any time, but if you want to make any sense of this as quickly as possible it won't kill you to stay until after to speak with her. I'll see you in the morning, Buttercup." The door clicked behind her and Abby was left alone in the giant bedroom. Setting the glass down, she pulled the heavy duvet down and crawled in becoming aware that Phoebe was right about needing rest when a deep yawn overcame her.

She felt silly leaving the lights on, she hadn't done that in a very long time, but being alone gave her a serious case of the creeps. Her thoughts drifted to Phoebe's words - *Pretty well any supernatural being you can think of. They're all real in a sense.* And they could all be walking the halls of this place right now. She expected to hear cackles and howls, at least claws scraping the walls. But it was eerily quiet around her. The wind outside had even stilled, the rustling of the leaves no longer curling through the dense forest below the window. Abby quickly realized that she had no idea how to get out of here if she wanted to, or worse, if she needed to. Based on the size of the only room she'd been in, it was a fair assumption that the rest of the manor was palatial. It was called a manor, after all. And she never really found out how she had gotten there, or what they had done with her all day. She hoped that they had just 'Sleeping Beautied' her and left her alone in this room. She was getting pretty sick of these Patrons knocking her out. Hopefully Phoebe would have answers more readily available tomorrow - especially what exactly she was. The way she skirted the issue with her made her consider the idea that maybe she didn't want to know. If all the monsters she'd ever thought were just stories are in fact real, couldn't that mean there are monsters even more frightening that she'd never heard of? She tried to put a list of questions for Gretchen together in her head for the morning but the exhaustion slowly crept over her, winning the battle against her heavy eyes.

Chapter 5

The trees seemed to reach past the sky when she was beneath them, blocking all but a few sunbursts that lit the trail in front of her. The smell of the forest was soothing, reminding Abby of hiking with her mother. Moss and wet dirt mingled through the sharp smell of the pine needles. She raised her face to a warm beam of sunshine, stopping to take a deep comforting breath.

"You always doddle for the right reasons, don't you Abby?" Her eyes shot open widening at the sound of her voice, her heartbeat thumping in her head.

"Mom?" she barely got the word out when her eyes locked on her mother, the exact rich emerald green that she remembered, peeking around a massive tree twenty feet away. She jumped over to the trail and closed the space between them in a blink, pulled Abby against her. She wrapped her shaking arms around her, her smell and tears overtaking her. "Mom, how are you here?"

"I'm always here baby girl. I'll always find you, Abby. And so will he. He loves you so much. You are loved, my baby, you are so very loved. Don't be afraid." She tripped forward when her arms slammed back across her chest. She spun around looking for her, running down the trail, tears soaked her cheeks. A dark shadow starting to nip at her heels before it started to crawl up her body, cold and sour smelling.

"Mom? Mom! Come back, please mom! I need you! Please!" Her throat burned with her shrieks but her voice was deadened against the thick forest around her and the shadow started to slow her.

"Not now Kieran. She needs to speak with Gretchen first – the same thing you should be doing now." Phoebe's hushed attempt at whispering filled the room pulling Abby awake. She could hear a muffled voice answer back before footsteps started away and disappeared. She wiped at tears that were spilling down her face and rolled to her side, sinking into the blankets. When she peeked up at the clock on the nightstand it showed her that she had slept in until almost noon.

"Pheebs?" Her voice was small and shaky from sleep and crying.

"Buttercup, you're up!" She turned, plastering on a big smile, until she saw her curled up wiping at tears. "What's wrong, Abby? What's happened?" She sat on the bed, rubbing Abby's arm.

"I saw my mom." Her comforting touch was making her voice a little stronger. "I saw her in the forest, Phoebe."

"Oh, honey, it was just a dream." She leaned down gathering her into her arms.

"But it felt so real! I could smell her and feel her arms around me. She was there, Pheebs! I've never had a dream feel so real. Ever." She pulled out of the hug and rolled onto her back, looking towards the window. The sunshine lit up the tops of the trees that were just shadows the night before. "She was really there." The smell of the trees still danced around her and an uneasy feeling of the cold shadow still tickled at her skin.

Phoebe's free hand made its way up to tangle a curl around her fingers, her eyes lost in thought. "Did she say anything to you?"

She smiled remembering her voice. "She was teasing me for doddling on the trail… and she hugged me." She could still feel her warm arms around her.

"Did she say anything else?"

Abby felt a tear slide down from the corner of her eye towards the pillow.

"She said I was loved and that she's always here. I'm being silly, you're right it was just a dream. It just felt so…." She could still smell the sweet lingering scent of her shampoo, the light vanilla perfume that she always wore. "She said he does too." Abby turned to meet her eyes. "She said he loves me too." Phoebe pursed her lips into a tight smile while she listened. "What do you think that means? Maybe my dad?"

Phoebe patted Abby's leg and stood from the bed. "It means get your butt out of bed and into the shower. It's time to go talk to your Grandmother. Meet me downstairs when you're ready, ok?"

Abby stretched her arms and legs as far as she could, waking herself and shaking off the dream. "So I'm allowed out of my cell today?"

Phoebe laughed looking around the room. "Ya, you've been real hard done by here. I don't know how you made it!" Abby stuck her tongue out at her and was flipped off with a smile in return.

"Just meet me downstairs, convict!" Phoebe yelled over her shoulder, heading down the hallway.

Abby tossed the covers back and stretched the full length of her body again before dragging herself out of the warm bed. She shuffled into the bathroom and took a quick shower before pulling a brush through her tangled mess of wet hair. Digging through her knapsack for clothes, she was unsure what she should wear for a sit down with 'The Queen of the Creatures'. Deciding on white shorts and her favorite well-worn navy blue college hoodie, she dressed and headed for the door. Pulling her long hair up into a ponytail, she stood outside the bedroom looking up and down the hall. *Now where would downstairs be?* The hallway stretched far past her in both directions, the shiny wooden floors partially covered by an elegant runner with tiny pale blue flowers dotted along it. There were half a dozen closed doors on either side of her. The light walls, that matched the ones in the bedroom, were covered with a mixture of old oil paint portraits, and stunning black and white photographs framed in ornate black frames. It was very cheery and warm, not like the palace décor she had been expecting. She headed to the right, the direction Phoebe had headed, figuring she had a 50/50 chance of finding some stairs. She came to the end of the hall and found a grand staircase that spiraled to a floor below. As she grazed her hand on the smooth handrail, feeling like an underdressed Scarlett O'Hara, she made her way down. The stairs opened to another similar looking floor with the exception of an impressive picture window opposite her that Kieran was sitting in, his long legs stretched out, crossed at the ankles. His blue eyes, as heart stopping as she remembered, turned to her from whatever held his attention out the window. He sat frozen in place, as if trying not to spook a timid animal. The sun glimmered in his hair, lighting him up from behind like a Botticelli angel.

"Abby…how are you feeling?" He slowly swung his socked feet to the floor with Abby still rooted in place on the last step staring at him. Stepping onto the floor she kept her hand on the railing – steading the nerves that he rattled whenever she saw him. He had a way of tugging up just half of a smile when looked at her that tightened something raw inside of her. It affected her in ways that it shouldn't, but she couldn't get enough of it. How could one man be so damn attractive?

"I'm ok. I'm good. A little overwhelmed and a lot confused, but good." He smiled and she couldn't help but smile back. A blush rushed to her cheeks making her eyes cast down, embarrassed that her emotions could play so easily on her face. "Why are you here?" She looked back up to meet his eyes when she was able to quell the silly schoolgirl that, apparently, lived in her mind and hormones now. Those eyes affected her in ways she couldn't understand.

"I live here." He smiled again, making the giggling schoolgirl take over Abby's mind once more.

"You live here? With my Grandmother?"

A radiant smile lit his face and he chuckled at her. "Well I don't live *with* your Grandmother. I just live in the Manor. A lot of us do."

"It does seem like it has room for a lot of people, I suppose…. is it rude to call you people?" Abby felt like an ass and a voice in head was telling her to just walk away before she truly embarrassed herself. "I don't know why I just asked you that."

Kieran stood up from the window, his head tilted, eyes on her, with that smile lighting up his face. "No *people* is fine. 'People' just means a group, a tribe. We're all people here – as are you." They stood on each side of the hallway staring at each other for a moment. "I'm truly happy you're here now, Abby."

She loved how he said 'Abby', how it could somehow sound affectionate. As if the word alone were a pet name that was between just them.

"Thanks." The only word she could muster. She felt tongue tied and ridiculous for it and steeled herself to be more rational. Although rational wasn't something she was seeing much of in the world around her lately. "So I'm supposed to go see my Grandma now." She looked around the hallway and noticed another set of stairs to the left, heading down, with Phoebe heading up.

"I was wondering what was keeping you." She spoke the words to Abby but her eyes were on him. "Kieran." She greeted him curtly.

"Phoebe." His lips twitched in that half smile, his eyes mischievous, before turning back to Abby. "I'm glad to see you're feeling better. I'll find you after you speak with your Grandmother and, hopefully, show you around. If you'd like."

"I can do th…" Phoebe's words were angry before being clipped by a glare from Kieran and she sighed. "I know, I know. Old habits." She linked arms with Abby and gave her a tug. "Come on Buttercup, no one leaves Gretchen waiting." She and Kieran shared a smile before he gave a quick nod and disappeared down another long hallway.

"Why don't you guys like each other?" She couldn't imagine any reason not to like him.

"It's not that we don't like each other, we just have different way of looking at things. But that doesn't matter anymore." She flashed a grin when they came to the bottom of the stairs, and led Abby across an enormous foyer to a set of large wooden doors and knocked.

"Come in dear." Gretchen's distinguished voice called from the other side.

Phoebe opened one of the heavy doors to a room with fluffy couches across from each other and walls of books that led to another large window overlooking Lake Constant. Abby's Grandmother sat behind an ancient looking desk that was carved with intricate details along the legs, her light gold hair still piled into a neat bun on top of her head and her hands crossed in front of her. The pale yellow cardigan she wore over a crisp white shirt made her appear less severe than the formal business suit she had on the day before. Her hand rose to her neck to straighten a small strand of pearls before smoothing her hair when she watched Abby follow Phoebe.

"Come in, Abigail, please. Sit." She motioned to the couches when she rose from behind the desk. Abby looked timidly to Phoebe who smiled and nodded, stepping behind her to give her a little push on the back before ducking out of the room. The door clicked shut behind her and she turned back to her Grandmother, who had perched herself on one of the plush couches. She cautiously moved to the opposite couch, nervously eying Gretchen, a woman who was not only a complete stranger to her but a woman who had the apparent ability to knock her unconscious and lose the memories of an entire day with some crazy supernatural granny powers. Although she looked nowhere near old enough to be a grown woman's grandmother. Another super power she mused to herself as she regarded her, looking just as nervous as she felt. She noticed Puccini's Nessum Dorma softly playing from unseen speakers when she sat. Memories of the opera's notes creeping out from the bathroom when her mom would play her Turandot record soaking in a bubble bath filled her heart.

"Well, here we are." She was surprised when a small, but genuine smile appeared on Gretchen's face. It gave a warm sense of family to her. "I believe you have many questions for me, however, I'd like to share some things with you before you begin." She paused for a reply, continuing when Abby nodded slightly. "Excellent." She took a slow breath and sat gracefully back into the couch, her hands clasped on her lap. "I am well aware of how difficult this is for you, and your feelings are not being taken lightly. I want to be aware of that fact. I will do my very best to help you to adjust to the changes, as well as the responsibilities that will fall to you and your place among us now. With that said, my dear, you cannot change who you are. There are things in this world that have been kept from you in the same manner that it has been kept from those you have been living amongst. When you mother left us…" She paused to take a small breath, her words were paced and thoughtful, the memory of her daughter clearly affecting her. "When she left us we were very much hurt. We didn't understand her decision, nor did we know that she had the ability to make such a choice." She rose from the couch, crossing to a small wet bar to pour a kettle of water into a teapot that she placed on a tray, bringing it to the table between the sofas. She sat a small black tea cup and saucer with delicate pink flowers painted around it in front of Abby. "Milk with two generous heaps of sugar, I believe?" She picked up the cup; dumbfounded after her Grandmother had prepared her tea exactly as she preferred it.

"Yes, how did you know that? Phoebe?" She looked down at the tea steaming in her hands.

"I have my ways." She smiled slightly, taking a small sip from her matching cup before setting it back on the saucer and sitting back on the couch to continue. "Patron's are very special, Abigail. We are special in the society in which we exist and we are extraordinary in the eyes of someone that lives outside of our world. Beyond that, our lives are carried out in a very different manner than those we watch over." Her fingers traced the pearls on her neck again. "If you were to think of insects, they live an existence that is completely separate from us. Or so we'd think. If you would consider bees for example, they have an impact on our lives far more than we give any thought to. But there they are. And here we are." Softness traced her face when she looked at her granddaughter. "Your mother was also different from us in a way that we had never experienced in our lifetimes. As we live, every Patron is born with a mate so to speak. Sometimes they are many years apart in age or many miles apart in home, with so many of us spanning the globe, but we will always find a way to our mate. We are born to have one and only one in this life." She leaned forward to sip her tea, her eyes trying to read Abby's face beyond the confused stare she projected at her.

"You mean like soul mates?"

"Something like that, yes. But we will always find our other; there is no question in that. The people you've been brought up with like that idea, to actually have that one special person in the universe meant solely for them alone. But it's rooted in us, in Patrons. It's a sort of fairytale of how we live, how we are. As Patron's there is no exception to what they romanticize, the idea of soul mates as you say.

Except your mother, your mother was… different. When she was born she had the mark of a Solitary, which is exceptionally rare. Do you remember the small mark on her hand?"

Abby nodded, remembering immediately the red mark below her mom's right pinky finger that looked like it could have been a burn or a birthmark depending on the answer she gave when asked.

"The teardrop scar?"

She smiled and closed her eyes. "That's a very suiting description of it, Abigail." Her eyes opened and gazed at her. "That mark is of a Patron that has been born to be with one not of our kind. A Solitary, and they are truly important to our way of life and position of power."

Abby picked up her tea so she'd have something to do with her hands other than wring them. *Not of our kind?* Her Grandmother mirrored her, picking up her cup, staring into it before continuing.

"There are many different people in this world, Abby, and not all of them are known to you as of right now. The world of the Supernatural beings live alongside the people you have been raised with, but rarely are we exposed to them. We have certain abilities that could be abused by those in that community, as well as some of us that could be a threat to them if we were to comingle. My daughter was born a Patron born to find a mate with one of another nature and that bond would make her of their blood, so to speak. We, as Patrons, are all strongly connected by our blood and a Solitary is what bonds our blood to the other natures that we oversee. The Solitary's bond becomes our bond. This in turn strengthens us and keeps us tied to the communities we oversee."

'But I thought my dad was just a regular guy." Abby didn't remember her dad having any special powers, although her mother never showed any sign of being anything more than she knew her to be either.

"Yes, dear, he was. Your mother fell in love with a Transient and that is something that is just not done. She had a responsibility to her family, and to her people, to make us all stronger and she chose to leave us. She chose to be with him instead." She quieted again, her attention moving to the window before she spoke again. "It was nothing we had ever dealt with before, a brief whispered story here and there of a defiant ancestor, from many hundreds of years ago, that may have done the same; however it was not something we were prepared to deal with." She placed her teacup on the table and rose from the couch again; walking towards the window she smoothed her sweater and then her hair. "When you arrived we weren't sure what to expect. If you would have any ties to us, or to here. We had no inkling if you were to be lost to us forever until we realized you were born with a Patron mate." She turned to face her, a smile lighting up her eyes.

Abby choked on her tea before setting it down with a clunk, spilling some drops on the table that she quickly soaked up with her sleeve, embarrassed. "I'm sorry, born with a mate?"

"Yes, my dear. We were quite unsure in the beginning; a Solitary Patron's children are not Patrons by blood. They take on the nature of the other parent."

"So then shouldn't I be just like my dad then?" That seemed like the most obvious answer to her, but seeing as she was sitting where she was, she figured she was wrong.

"That is precisely what we had all expected. Until Kieran."

"You're telling me that Kieran is my soul mate?" Her stomach flipped at the idea.

"It would appear so."

"Shouldn't I feel that then?" As soon as she spoke the words she thought of the reaction she had to just being near him. The bumbling words, the blushed cheeks, the intense need to feel his lips on hers. She blinked rapidly a few times, shaking her head a bit to bring her mind back to the conversation at hand.

"That, my darling, is the part we are still figuring out. As I've said, your mother was somewhat unique, but you? You are more than unique. You are one of a kind. But…" She pondered her thought, making her way back to the couches and sat gingerly beside her granddaughter, the smell of her perfume was the exact warm vanilla of Lucy's. "I am quite curious of your feelings towards Kieran."

"I barely know him. I met him two days ago. How could I have feelings for someone I don't know?" She avoided her grandmother's eyes, as if she'd be able to look inside her mind and see the ever-growing thoughts she had of him.

"Do you find yourself at all drawn to him? Romantically perhaps?" She sat slightly back against the arm of the sofa. "Do you find him in your thoughts?"

"He's gorgeous, of course I notice him. He's kind of hard to miss."

Gretchen smiled widely for a moment before composing herself. She rose to take her seat across from Abby again, a smile twitching on her lips as she raised her teacup to them.

"So you're telling me Kieran has no choice but to love me?" Not exactly a romantic prospect in her opinion. Her sweaty hands tucked up into the sleeves of her sweatshirt.

"It's as much a choice as breathing. We weren't sure if it could be true, at first. But when you know, my darling, you just know. And he knew." Abby's heart picked up pace at the idea that Kieran could actually be destined for her, to have feelings that strongly for her. "The only suffering that can come from our love is to be denied close proximity to our mate. This was, unfortunately, something that was happening to Kieran and the reason that you are here now. I cannot compel you to stay with anything other than that knowledge. You are free to go at anytime but I want you to have the knowledge that your actions affect us all. All I ask of you is a few days to learn your mother's – and your own – history. Spend some time with us, time that we have been denied for so long. Give your sweet Granny some time to get to know you." She smiled brightly at her when she muffled a laugh. To call this stunning woman standing before her, looking maybe twenty years older than Abby herself, a granny was laughable. "But mostly spend some time with Kieran. Humor us."

Abby didn't hate the idea of that, but she didn't think she could just disappear from home for several days without someone asking questions. "Can I call my Aunt and Uncle?"

"Of course you can. You can speak with them whenever you want, as long as you tell them nothing of what I've told you. You would be putting all of us in danger – Thomas, Julie and yourself included."

"They must be worried that I haven't called." She reached into her pocket to fish out her cellphone. No new calls or messages. Her brow furrowed at the screen.

"As far as they are aware, Phoebe and yourself are spending the week in the city at a friend's home. You're there to look for apartments." She flicked her eyebrow up with a pleased smile.

Abby added about twenty more questions to the list of things she wanted to ask her Grandmother but felt she'd absorbed enough information for one sitting. She considered what she was being asked.

"So you just want me to stay for a few days? No strings attached?"

"No strings attached."

It didn't seem like the worst way to spend a few days, especially having Phoebe there with her. *And Kieran – oh god, how awkward was it going to be with Kieran now?* She took a deep breath and slowly nodded her head.

"Ok. I'll stay for a few days."

Gretchen clasped her hands and blazed a smile. "Oh my darling, I'm so pleased to hear that. Thank you." Abby smiled at her weakly, not really sure what was in store for her.

"Now, would you like to ask me any questions?"

Abby had to chuckle at that. "No I think I have enough to think about for now, if that's alright." She rubbed her head trying to process everything she was just told.

"That's quite fair. You may come to me with anything you'd like to discuss whenever you need, Abigail. We're so very pleased to have you in our lives after so long."

"Ok, thank you. I'd like to go get some air now if that's alright." She stood from the couch and returned her phone to her pocket.

"Of course, my dear. Take your time with all you're being told. I truly do understand how overwhelmed you must be. I'd like for you to join us for dinner tonight, if you would. Your Grandfather is very much looking forward to making your acquaintance."

"I'd like that. Thank you." Abby left her and clicked the giant door behind her to find Phoebe sprawled sideways across an enormous armchair in the foyer; her legs draped over one arm, her shock of red hair hanging over the other. She jumped to her feet when she saw her.

"So are you staying?" her excitement rolled off of her, waiting for an answer

"I am." Abby smiled at her when she started jumping up and down squealing. "But only for a few days."

"I'll take it! This is awesome!" She threw her arms around her, still jumping up and down.

"Calm down spazzy." Her enthusiasm made her smile even more, feeling less shaky from what she'd been told. "For all that you said about not wanting me know about all of this, you seem surprisingly glad that we're staying."

"Well, I can think of worse ways to relax for a few days, is all. We couldn't afford to go away on break last year and the wine cellar here more than makes up for that."

She certainly wasn't wrong. "Can we go outside for a bit?"

"Anything you want, Buttercup!" She picked up the handles of a bulky paper bag that was leaning against the armchair, before taking Abby's hand and tugging her along through tall glass doors, out past a long stone porch and onto a lush green lawn. From the outside the house was even more impressive, styled like a small castle. Small being a relative term for the biggest house she'd ever seen outside of movies, with detailed stone work and wrought iron windows overlooking expansive grounds covered in gardens, ancient trees rocketing to the sky and stone pathways so long you couldn't see the end of them. They followed one around the Manor to the lake that was sparkling almost aquamarine in the warm June sun, the forest wrapping around the far side and rising up the mountainous hills. Phoebe took them down to the waterside, sitting at the end of a dock in chairs that sunk them into plush cushions. They both sighed when they raised their faces to the sunshine. Phoebe rifled through the paper bag, pulling out small bottles of pink smoothies and two big fruit cups.

"I figured you would be starving by now. I have some of the Danishes you like in here too, if you want."

Abby took a fruit cup and smoothie from her, popping the cap and taking a sip. "Ugh, I'm still full from the hundred pounds of cheese on the nachos last night. Please tell me one of the superpowers you guys have is burning calories."

Phoebe giggled, swallowing a mouth full of melon. "Lucky for you it is!" She waved her finger around as if it was a magic wand "Abraca-gym! It's called a gym, lazy ass."

"Well what's the point of having magic powers if you can't put them to good use?"

She attempted to feign annoyance with her. "Who said anything about magic powers? This isn't wizard school, Abby."

"You're right, mind control and secret societies of supernatural beings is super normal. Why would I think there could be magic powers involved? "Phoebe punched her arm lightly and Abby popped a grape in her mouth. "So…what are you?" She seemed just as Abby was in her opinion, except for her confidence – although, knowing what she knows now, she wasn't so average anymore. She curled up in the chair, turning to face her.

"I think you may have heard enough to fill your head for one day." She stared off at the lake when she spoke.

"No, seriously, I want to know. If I'm a Patron, or half a Patron… or related to Patrons – if I'm whatever the hell a Patron is, what are you?"

She twisted her mouth, considering the words, before turning to Abby. "Ok then." She held her hands out and smiled. "I'm a Banshee."

"What? You're a what?" She barely got the words out between giggles. "You're a Banshee?"

"I am. I'm a Banshee." She smiled proudly.

"Bullshit." Abby sat straight up in her chair. "You're an actual Banshee?"

"Yep. Full blood, real life Banshee."

"So you can fly? Oh my god, do you kill people?" She started to get a little creeped out – *how could her best friend be a monster?* She immediately hated that she thought that about her.

It was Phoebe's turn to laugh now. "No I can't fly and no I don't kill people. What you read in books isn't exactly factual. And for good reason."

"So what do you do then? Don't you have any special powers?"

Phoebe stilled and turned back to the lake, her eyes shadowed, all traces of laughter gone. "I'm a Harbinger of Death. I can see death approaching someone." Her voice was small; she looked down at her fingers that were twisting each other. "But I don't kill anyone."

"Seriously? That's awful. It's no wonder you didn't want to come back here." The thought of her cheery friend having all of those dark thoughts inside her head broke her heart.

She pushed up a weak smile. "Being away from here didn't change who I was, Abby. It just gave me a chance to pretend I was different. I was trying to be like you, which was my biggest mistake because you're just like me – you just didn't know it yet."

Dragging her hands under her eyes to wipe away tears that refused to fall, she sat up in her chair and cleared her throat. "We all have shit to deal with and putting it in someone else's pile doesn't make it go away." She laughed hollowly.

"So your parents are Banshees too? I thought that only girls could be Banshees?" She wasn't sure if she wanted to hear any more, but curiosity got the best of her. It wasn't every day that your best friend tells you she a damn Banshee.

"Like I keep telling you, Abby, we're not like the stories you've read. My parents are both Banshees, my dad is just…different from my mom and I."

"How is he different?" Abby could feel Phoebe starting to get uncomfortable with the questions but she couldn't help herself.

"Female Banshees sense death, like when it's coming, and Males are the Consorts of Death." Her eyes drifted back out to the lake, following a seagull that skimmed along the surface.

"What does that mean? Consort?"

"It means sometimes death needs a little help and that's what he does." Her voice was quick and agitated. "I don't want to talk about my family right now, Abby. I'm sorry, I just…" Her voice trailed off when she looked up over at her curious friend's face. Abby could see that she was pained with the interrogation. She knew she should know better than to push the subject of her family and reached over to rub her tiny shoulder, giving her an apologetic smile. "Don't give me that sympathetic look you do. I know what I am and I'm very aware of what my family is, but I can't focus on the negative parts. The bad things always pass. They always have and they always will. Just like a fart. And who wants to focus on a fart?"

"Did you just compare your family to a fart?"

"Well just the bad parts of my family."

Abby cracked up with laughter. "Well at least the Banshee explains your hair!" She tugged lightly on a lock of her bright auburn hair, trying to lighten the mood.

Phoebe threw a blueberry from her cup at her and laughed. "Screw you, man!" her face relaxed into a smile again. "Ya, they got that part right in the stories, didn't they?" she twirled a lock in front of her eyes. "I'm really impressed with how well you're taking all of this, you know."

"I think it might all be *so* crazy that it has to be believed. Does that make sense?" She dug through her fruit cup until she found a big piece of pineapple.

"I think so." Phoebe smiled and nodded. Her eyes swung over to her in a flash, a Cheshire grin spreading across her pale face. "Soooo… what did Gretchen tell you about Kieran?" Abby shoved the giant slice of pineapple in her mouth and smiled at her, cheeks full. "Nuh-uh! Nice try. Seriously, how much did she tell you?" She pretended she was going to pinch her arm. "Tell me! How long until you can tell me what he looks like naked?"

Abby spit out the mouthful of fruit that she was suddenly choking on. "Oh my god, Phoebe! I thought you hated him." She kicked the chewed up fruit into the lake and smacked her arm.

"Nah, I've never hated him – I just hated that he was taking away our happy little life. I actually spent a lot of time running around in the woods with him and the other kids before I came to live in town. He's a great guy, Abby. Seriously. Now what did she tell you? What all did you talk about?" She tossed her fruit cup into the bag and pulled out a Danish, ripping a big chunk off.

"I don't know, she was talking about how we're meant to be together and bees and my parents and…"

"Bees? Your grandmother gave you the sex talk?" Phoebe gaped at her with a full mouth of pastry.

"No, it's not – not the birds and the bees. She was talking about how things live beside things and how we don't notice them and stuff. But she told me that Kieran was born to be with me. I think that could be the weirdest thing I've been told about all of this so far."

"I have to agree with that, for sure. That's always been strange to me." Phoebe pulled her sunglasses from her collar and slid them on, stretching her legs out in front of her to tan.

"So you don't do that? You don't…"

"No we have complete free will in the love department. At least free will compared to you guys. We usually end up with other Banshees, I guess. It's easier to relate to someone who knows exactly what you have to do. It's pretty well the only way to make little Banshees bambinos, too. When we're with someone outside of our nature it can be almost impossible to get pregnant and when you do it's not like it's a perfect little blend of both parents. They take after either their mother or father, never both." Abby sat silently as she dug around in her fruit cup. "As weird as it is that Patron's don't have a choice in who they love, I think it's kinda nice, you know?" She took another bite and spoke through her mouthful, "A guaranteed true love – now that's a free will I'd give up to have a piece of that. So much less work." She smiled after cramming another piece into her mouth.

"Well with manners like that, there's no wonder you have so many suitors!" Abby laughed at the monkey face she made with her full cheeks. "I don't know how any of that applies to me though.

How can he have feelings like that for me? We don't know each other. We've barely spoken."

"Don't ask me. If you're a mystery to all of them, there is no way I'd understand it." She pulled her legs up underneath her and twirled her hair in front of her face again. "As awkward as it is, maybe the best way is to just spend some time with him. Maybe something's there, maybe something's not – either way you're here now. You've been pretty accepting of everything so far, so would it be a stretch to hang out with a gorgeous guy who can also answer more questions than I ever possibly could?" She flicked her hair to the side and raised her eyebrows to her.

"I guess you're right. But, for now, I think I'm going to call Aunt Julie and check in." She stood up from the cozy chair and stretched her hands above her, taking in the beautiful views around the lake.

"Did Gretchen tell you what they told them? About where you are – or should I say where you're supposed to be?"

"She did, and I guess that's for the best. Not that they'd believe the truth anyways. I just want to hear her voice, have some semblance of normalcy before dinner with my brand new magic Grandparents tonight."

Phoebe laughed, grabbing the bag and the empty containers before standing up beside her. "I'll give you some privacy. Tell them I say hello." She rubbed Abby's arm when she passed by heading back up towards the house. She turned to shout over her shoulder, "Come and find me before dinner!" before she disappeared around the large stonewall.

Abby pulled her phone from her pocket and stared at the screen. It had been less than 48 hours since she last spoke to them but it felt like a lifetime. Everything she knew of her life had changed, including her relationship with the two people that had tried so hard to make her feel normal again when her parents had passed. She knew it was pointless to call them when she had to play along with the crazy mind washing they had done to them but none of that mattered at the moment, she just needed to hear their voices. She punched in the house number and sat down on the edge of the chair, her nerves were ridiculously rolling through her stomach.

"Hey Sweetie! How's the big city treating you guys?" She sounded as normal as ever. No inkling of the insanity that had become her niece's world.

"Hey Aunt Julie, it's good. It's good here. Pheebs says hi." Abby's voice sounded stronger than she expected.

"Hi to Phoebe! Are you guys having fun?"

"Yeah, it's…it's certainly different here." There's the understatement of her life.

"Oh please, Abby. Don't let that concrete jungle intimidate you now that you're not in school. You've been outside of that campus more than once. Just make sure you both pick an apartment that you love and can afford. Are you sure you don't want me to come down and be an impartial vote?"

"No! No. Thank you Aunt Julie, we're good." Abby didn't want to have to go tell her grandmother that Julie was wandering the city looking for them.

"Ok. My big girls taking on the city, you make me feel old." Her laugh tugged at her heart. It felt wrong to lie to her even though she had no idea what was really happening. "Have you found anything that seems like a fit for you both yet?"

"We're, uh…still looking. Nothing we want to nail down yet." It felt so wrong lying to her.

'Well, Thomas will be down that he wasn't here to hear from you. He's at the golf course with the boys. Are you sure you don't need anything, sweetie? We're just a quick car ride away, you know."

"No, I'm… we're good Aunt Julie. I just wanted to check in, how are you guys?" She started to pace on the dock. She wanted so badly to tell her how not good she really was, but Gretchen's words of the danger that they could be placed in rang in her head. She'd shared everything with Julie, for as long as she could remember and just like that she had that intimacy taken away from her. It occurred to her that she might be trading one family for another if she chose to stay with her mother's family.

"Oh you know we're good, Abby. Missing you but it's worth it. We're so proud of you, Abby." She could tell from her voice she was misting up with the happy tears that flooded her eyes so often.

"Thank you so much for all that you've done for me, Aunt Julie. I appreciate everything and love you both so much." Now her eyes were starting well up. She stared at the water lapping against the dock, trying to distract herself from sounding too emotional.

"Anything we can do for you we're here. Are you ok, Abby?"

"I am. I'm good. I love you guys. I have to go but I'll check in again soon, ok?" She wanted to tell her all of the incredible things that had happened in the last couple of days and knew she had to hang up before she couldn't stop herself from telling her everything. She never could keep secrets from her, but that had never been a problem until now.

"Ok, sweetie. Be safe, ok? I love you."

"I will. Love you too. Talk soon." She pushed end before she started to cry. Hearing the familiar sound of her voice made her want to forget about all of this craziness. All she could hope was that if she couldn't handle all of this, she could go back to the life she had with them and her dusty research at the museum. She wondered if Gretchen could just hocus pocus away all what she'd been told, and what she had seen, so she could leave it all behind as if it had never happened. But she had told her that her actions impact all of them now, and that didn't make it seem like she could just walk away. But for now all she could focus on was a nice long bath in that amazing tub in her room. She made her way back up the pathway, the last of the lilacs still filling the air with their sweet fragrance, and headed back inside. Opening the heavy glass door, she slipped inside. It was very quiet for a house that seemed all together made for echoes. She had one foot on the steps when she noticed someone rounding the stairs from the second floor. He slowed his step when he caught sight of Abby, a boyish grin spreading across his face.

"Well, here we are then - you must be Abby!" She could hear a slight trace of a British accent in his words and he appeared to be in his late 20's. His warm brown eyes were large and friendly and they seemed to sparkle when he spoke. "We've been waiting quite some time to meet you, young lady."

Hopping down the rest of the stairs he stood next to her. His pale skin seemed creamy against rich coffee shaded hair and he was dressed casually in grey cargo shorts topped with a white henley shirt.

"I'm very pleased to meet you, my dear. I'm Marcus." He mocked a slight bow before extending his hand. She reached out to shake it when she noticed his friendly smile was complete with 2 shiny white fangs. Her hand froze as she stared at his mouth. "My goodness, do I have the pleasure of being your first of my kind?" His smile widened, showing the full length of his gleaming incisors. She remembered her manners and shook his hand - it wasn't cold like she had expected.

"I'm sorry, yes you are - my first." She pulled her hand back and crossing her arms.

"Oh my, I like the sound of that!" He raised his eyebrows and his eyes were dancing with mischief.

"I'm...um..." She didn't know how to reply to that, so she just awkwardly smiled at him.

"I'm teasing you, sweetheart." He put his hands up in front of himself as a sign of peace. "I'm harmless, I swear." His smile was fanged but friendly; Phoebe was right, no one here was like the stories.

"No, I know, I mean - I'm sorry. All of this is a little..."

"I could only imagine, love. You're a lot for us to take in as well." He put his hand on her shoulder, giving a sympathetic grin. "You'll adjust soon enough. But we will have to become better acquainted at another time as I'm off." He turned for the door.

"So you can go outside? During the day I mean." Abby couldn't decide if it was rude or not to ask.

"Of course I can, love! Not everything dark lives in the shadows." He flashed her another bright grin and winked before opening the door. "It was truly enchanting to meet you."

The door shut behind him and she climbed the stairs to her third floor room. The late afternoon sun shone through the window at the far end of the hall, lighting most of the hallway brightly. She strolled along admiring the charming photographs along the walls; moments of nature beautifully captured in black and white. She stopped at one when she recognized Lake Constant. It looked as if it was awash in diamonds the way the sunlight sparkled across the water and standing on the very dock she had just returned from was her mother. She was much younger than she could have remembered but she was sure it was her; hands on her hips, smiling face raised to the camera. She felt a pang of sadness slam into her gut. This was the first actual evidence of her mother having a life here at one time; proof of her life as a Patron.

    She made her way to her room and into the ensuite to start a bath - which was exactly what she needed. Sitting on the edge of the giant tub she stared out onto the lake and trees below. Closing her eyes, she pictured her beautiful mom smiling in the sunshine, with no idea of what lay ahead for her in the world. She got up to grab her body wash and loofah from the counter, and set them on a thin wooden shelf that sat across one end of the tub. Slipping out of her clothes and into the warm bath water she felt herself relax almost instantly. She pulled a cloth from the tray, soaked it in the hot water and laid it over her eyes, trying to imagine what it would have been like if she had grown up here; always knowing about what her mother and her family were. What she was. She wondered if her Grandparents shunned her mother when she fell in love with her father, or did she choose to stay away to protect him from the bogeymen that she lived among? Did she really love her dad so much that she would put him, his whole family really, in danger of being too close to these people? Did she consider what that could mean for Abby's life or her future and would she have told her about all of this if she had lived longer, long enough to see Abby become a woman?

    She slopped some body wash on the loofah and scrubbed it on her neck, taking in a long slow breath, her nose was filled with the sweet floral scent. The warm water eased her mind that was scrambled with all of the things that had become her new reality, taking her away from it all until the tub turned cool. She wrapped herself in a giant towel and pulled a smaller one from rack to twist up around her hair. The backpack wasn't on the side table, where she had left it earlier, so she wandered out into the bedroom in search of her clothes. A smaller door beside the bed led to an enormous walk in closet filled with racks and drawers, a small crystal chandelier lighting up the space. A portion of her meager wardrobe was hanging up in the far corner - more of her clothes than had been in her backpack. She didn't want to know how the clothes had been retrieved from her tiny closet at home but beside the hangers was her fluffy purple robe that was begging to be worn. Tugging it off of the hook she bundled herself into it, hanging her damp towel on the doorknob. After grabbing her brush and cell phone from the bathroom she curled up on the bed. A remote control was on the nightstand and Abby picked it up, and started pressing the buttons, aiming all over the room. A giant landscape painting opposite her appeared to roll up into the wall revealing a huge TV that flicked on.

"You got to be frigging kidding me." Abby flicked through until she found the History Channel.

The clock on the nightstand was showing just after 5 and she realized she had no idea when she was supposed to have dinner with her Grandparents - or where they'd be. She picked up her phone to text Phoebe to see if she had any idea when there was a knock on the door.

"Well speak of the devil! Entrer!" She shouted in her horrible attempt at a French accent. The door opened a crack and Kieran's head peeked in, an adorable smirk on his face.

"French? Impressive." He stifled a laugh before his eyes landed on her robe, that wasn't exactly tightly closed above her cleavage, and then quickly shot them to the ground in front of him. "I'm so sorry, I'll come back later. "

She tugged the fabric closer around her neck but smiled at his embarrassment. His cheeks were flushed and his eyes were darting around the floor as if he had walked in on her completely nude.

"No it's ok, come in." His eyes stayed fixed on Abby's as he took a small step through the doorway. His eyes were so arresting, a blue that seemed to glisten, sparkling almost as if they were jeweled.

Abby realized that must be a Patron trait. His eyes were just like sapphires in the same way her mothers were emeralds.

"I don't want to intrude, but your Grandmother sent me to let you know dinner is at 7 on the rear patio." His eyes drifted up and down her slightly before snapping back to hers.

"Oh, ok." Something tugged inside of her at the sweet way he regarded her. There was certainly heat in his gaze but there was more - a longing perhaps. If it was true that he was meant to be with her, she believed she most certainly could do worse. He turned to leave but everything in her body wanted him to stay. She hit mute on the remote. "Wait… did you want to hang out a bit… before dinner?"

His broad smile answered the question. Opening the door all the way he stepped inside, giving the room a quick survey before deciding on one of the wing chairs under the window. He sat down and fussed with the seams on his shorts, before raking his hand nervously through his hair.

"So here we are." His voice was filled with nervous humor. Abby didn't know what to say; just being alone with him, watching him watching her, made her feel as if she'd never had feelings for a guy before now. But to be alone with him - in a bedroom - in nothing but a robe made her cheeks heat when she smiled at the situation. "I heard that you agreed to stay for a while."

"It looks that way. My grandmother wants me to spend some time with them so she asked me to stay for a few days."

"I'm assuming your conversation with Gretchen also included some mention of me?" His voice sounded smaller than the short times they'd spoken, almost shy.

"It did. We did - talk about you."

"So how freaked out are you right now?" It didn't seem like nervous laughter in his words now, he seemed to genuinely understand the absurdity of where they found themselves.

"Not so much freaked out as confused, really. It's a pretty bizarre thing to be told."

He jokingly grimaced, but kept his smile. "I can believe that. I've kind of been a walking freak show around here for years." She hadn't considered the idea that he was as unusual as her around here, and he'd been raised in this real life penny dreadful.

"Does it make it more strange now that I'm here?" She started to pull her brush through tangled hair to give her hands something to do with the discomfort she felt with a conversation that had to happen – sooner rather than later.

"For me? Truthfully it's much better...obviously." He shifted nervously in his seat. "I mean, a pair of weirdo's is more fun than one standing alone, wouldn't you say?"

"There is a power in numbers, I suppose, right?" She had an inner cringe at her dorkability, but when she looked at Kieran he had such a sweet look set on her. She marveled at how the laws of whatever may govern a Patron could force him to love her without knowing anything about her. But how could she not fall desperately head first for a man that could look at her like that. "So, my Grandmother thinks we should spend some time together. They don't quite know what to make of us weirdoes." She set her brush down and dragged her fingers through her less knotted hair, wishing she had saved the conversation for when she was a little more put together. She twisted her hair up in an elastic and turned to see an elated expression set on Kieran's face.

"Well no one says no to Gretchen, even Erick knows better."

"What's he like?"

"He's a great man." There was an honest reverence in his words. "He really is. All of us take pride in how he leads us."

"Leads you? I thought all the Patrons were the leaders... of the...you know, all the other people?"

Kieran smiled at the flustered way she tried to find the right words. "It so strange that you don't know any of this. I don't mean to sound insensitive, but this is so... strange to me." He came to sit on the edge of the bed opposite Abby. "It's nice to have someone else to talk to about it but I really do need to remember that this is all new to you, though." He paused to gather his thoughts. "Patron's aren't exactly leaders of the people; each nature has it's own leader but we're the ones that hold them all together. But we have our own governance, as Patrons, and that would be your Grandparents. Does that make sense?" His brow furrowed as he tried to explain.

"It does, I guess. I really can't believe there was a whole world living along side me my entire life and I had no idea of any of it. And my mother knew everything."

"Your mother was protecting you from something even she didn't understand. The three of us are pretty usual in a world that's already very exceptional from what you were raised in. You and your parents are fascinating; it's a pretty famous story around here." His face softened as he silently pondered something, his lips turned up slightly. "It's the best example I have of what I can hope for in my life."

The setting sun was casting shadows across the room and Abby reached over to switch on the lamp set on the nightstand. She turned back to him to find him watching the glowing burst of sun sinking behind the trees, seemingly lost in thought. The warmth of the light lit his face softly and she stole the moment to regard him without the effect of his gaze on her.

"I really am glad you're here. You have no idea how much better everything is with you here." His eyes stared out the window while he spoke before he turned back to her. "Abby I have no idea how you feel about everything you've been told in the last few days and I have no idea if any of us understand how things have changed now, for all of us, having you even exist. The only thing I do know is that our attachment is one hundred percent real for me and I was born to love you." He held his finger up when she tried to respond. "No, please, just let me say this – I've waited my entire life to say this to you. If I scare you away so be it because I need to say it. I've imagined every possible scenario that could come from every word I could speak to you and now that I finally have the chance…just let me, please." He made his way around the bed and lightly sat beside her. "I've been told that when your mother met your father her heart bonded to his – that's something that almost never happens, not with transients. Whatever it is that makes the attachments in us doesn't affect them, but the love your father had for your mother connected them in a way no one could understand." He paused, searching her face for understanding. "I thought that I would be alone for my entire life, wanting a girl I'd never know, but what happened with your parents gave me hope. Hope that things aren't always as we expect them to be and there was a chance that you and I could be an exception to the rule like your parents were. When everyone realized that I was meant for you, no one knew what to do with me. So I waited. And I will always wait because I don't have any other choice. But now that you're here, right here, I know that I'm perfectly happy just to be near you."

Abby reached out and took his hand. She knew the things he was saying should sound crazy to her, that it should frighten her. The warmth of their hands gingerly clasp sent a bolt straight from her chest down to her stomach, making her breath catch. He looked down at their hands, twining his fingers with hers. His mouth tried to form his thoughts into words before Abby spoke up.

"I don't know what this is, and I don't know how I feel the way I do, but what I do know is that I feel something. For you. Something that I've never felt before."

He reached up to her face, his fingers barely grazing her cheek. A small smile crept across his handsome face as he looked at her, taking in every inch of her own. She felt herself leaning forward, feeling the heat from his lips. His hand became firm on her cheek as the other released her hand and snaked up into her hair, pushing into her kiss. The scorch from their lips spread down Abby's body when his tongue slowly slid across hers, his hands holding her in place as if she could disappear at any moment. Her lips felt cold when he suddenly pulled away, nose to nose and his eyes locked with hers, his gaze filled with heat but searching for her reaction. Abby smiled shyly to his relief.

"Well that's definitely one the scenarios I had hoped for." His grin took over his face as he gently rubbed his nose on hers before sitting back and Abby became very aware that she was only wearing a robe, pulling it tightly at her neck. "I should let you get dressed for dinner." He stood up from the bed, biting his lip to keep his grin under control. He leaned down to press his lips to her forehead. "This is all up to you, Abby. I'll take things as slow as you want, as long you'll give me a chance. No matter what happens, you just made me happier than you could ever imagine." He hooked her chin with his thumb to turn her smile up to him. "I'll see you at dinner, ok?"

Words were still failing her so she replied with nod, her smile matching his. He walked over to doorway and turned to flash a dazzling smile as he shut the door. Laughter bubbled out of her when she heard him cheer loudly from down the hall. She touched her lips, still feeling the kiss as she walked over to the closet to get dressed.

## Chapter 6

Abby pulled on a light grey cotton maxi dress and shrugged on a long black cardigan when she remembered they were eating outside. After taking a blow dryer to her hair that had mostly air dried, she decided on a ponytail to wrangle it. She looked herself over in the bathroom mirror, wishing she had asked Phoebe if she needed to dress up for dinner here. She pulled her hair out of the elastic, trying to make it smoother and pulled it up again with the same result. She blew a breath out at her reflection, put on some mascara and slicked on her favorite lip-gloss, deciding she was too nervous to bother fussing. She opened the bedroom door just as Phoebe had raised her hand to knock, almost taking a thump to the head before she stopped herself.

"Well how's that for timing, you ready to eat? The table's all set in the gazebo for your welcome home dinner. I hope you're…" Her words trailed off as her eyes narrowed on Abby. "Holy shit! You slept with him!"

"What?" She felt her eyes widen, her cheeks heating up.

"Kieran – you slept with him didn't you?" She pushed her back into the bedroom and kicked the door shut behind her. "Holy shit! That was fast!" She looked like an over sugared child the way she was bouncing up and down, clapping her hands.

Abby stumbled back into the room backwards. "Oh my god, Phoebe! I did not sleep with him!"

Phoebe squared her eyes on her, her eyebrow popped up.

"I didn't I swear! Why would you even think that I did?"

"Because, you love struck hussy, you're absolutely glowing! It's all over your face!" She grasped Abby's face in her hands and made kissy faces.

"I swear we didn't have sex. We didn't!" Abby felt his lips on hers and heat spread across her body again.

"Holy hell – look at you. Something absolutely did happen. Spill." She threw herself sideways across the wing chair and pointed to the one beside her. Abby stayed put, hands on her hips. "Oh don't be coy. Spill."

"We just talked about some stuff." She couldn't understand how she could have known anything happened at all, but Phoebe did have a sixth sense when it came to guys.

Phoebe crossed her arms and popped her eyebrow again. "Aaand?"

"And we kissed, ok?" She tried to toss the word nonchalantly but she could feel her face flush again. Phoebe sat sprung straight up in the chair.

"You kissed? Seriously? That's it?" Her eyes were wide with surprise.

"You looked more shocked that we just kissed than when you thought we'd had sex!"

Her mouth silently mouthed 'wow'. "You just look…I don't know, you're glowing. Your eyes have a sparkle in them that I've never seen before. It must have been one hell of a kiss." She grabbed Abby's hand, pulling herself up from the chair and linked their arms. "Maybe this will turn out better than I thought. Let's go eat."

Abby followed her out into the hall and down the stairs to the foyer where they walked around to a huge sitting room behind the staircase. Two worn looking deep brown love seats sat opposite with an enormous matching couch running between them and the biggest TV she'd ever seen was mounted on the wall they faced. The dark trim and floors matched the rest of the house, but lush, deep red curtains that framed sliding glass doors and antique-looking elegant oil portraits made the room feel more opulent than the rest of the Manor that she had been in. They made their way out through the sliding doors and into the cool evening air, where the sun was just disappearing below the horizon. A stone pathway, lit with tiny inlayed lights, took them through a newly bloomed garden to steps leading up to a wooden gazebo overlooking the lake. Abby followed Phoebe up the trail; tucking herself behind her as they walked, she suddenly felt very shy. The thought of meeting her mother's dad for the very first time and to be in the same space with Kieran again made her a jumble of nerves. As if sensing her apprehension, Phoebe reached her arm around her back for Abby to take her hand. Abby was so grateful to have her there with her – she couldn't imagine any of this happening without her.

The table was set elegantly with white linen covering a round table large enough to seat at least ten, beautiful flowered china with sparking crystal glassware and gleaming silverware at each place. Thomas and Gretchen were already seated but her Grandfather rose from his seat when he saw them approaching. Smoothing his thick salt and pepper hair, he was tall and fit, and looked to be in his late fifties. Dressed smartly in a deep blue polo shirt tucked neatly into khaki pants, he had brilliant chestnut eyes flecked with gold, a warm smile on his lips. But when he looked at Abby it was as though he were looking through her, lost in thought before Gretchen cleared her throat quietly. He blinked quickly a few times before finding his voice.

"Abby it is so wonderful to have you here with us, at last." He spoke with a posh English accent that made her picture him at Eton or Oxford. "We've been looking forward to this for a very long while." He closed the space between them quickly and took her hands, looking her up and down. "Goodness, you are the picture of your mother." His smiled again brightly and gestured to the table. "Please sit. Phoebe, you are looking lovely as always." He winked at her and she turned her blush to the floor before taking a seat beside me. Abby's grandfather was apparently a bit of a charmer.

"Thank you so much for having me here. It's so beautiful." She looked out at the moon starting to rise behind the trees, a spray of stars taking over the sky, casting a reflection on the lake that was completely stunning.

"I've told your Grandfather that you've agreed to stay with us for a few days and he's as delighted as I am." Abby's grandmother raised her hand and signaled an older woman who appeared with a bottle of wine and attended to the glasses. Abby recognized her as the woman who came into her room with Barnaby the night before.

"Thank you, Maggie." Gretchen nodded to her when she approached.

Abby smiled warmly and thanked her when she filled her glass. The woman's cloudy blue eyes were friendly and crinkled in the corners when she smiled before disappearing back down the steps.

"Thank you so much for having me as well, Mr. and Mrs. Ambrose. I couldn't imagine not being here for Abby right now." Phoebe slid her hand over to hers, giving a reassuring squeeze when she looked at her.

"Oh nothing at all, my dear. Gretchen and I are grateful for all you've done for our Abby." It was strange hearing someone she had met only moments ago refer to her as 'our Abby'. It was nice to feel a part of a family that she had always wanted, but strange nonetheless. "Have you been showing her around the Manor today?"

"We had lunch on the dock today, but we haven't had a chance for a tour yet."

"I'd be happy to show her around tomorrow if she's free." Abby's heart thumped in her chest when she heard Kieran voice behind her and her attention turned to him when he sat down beside her at the table, his intense indigo eyes fixed on her before turning to her Grandparents. "I'm sorry for being late, I was catching up with my parents."

Gretchen motioned for Maggie to come back – which was wonderful because the little sips Abby thought she was politely taking were actually draining her glass and flushing her cheeks. Maggie, the wine fairy, filled Kieran's glass and thanked her politely before raising it to Abby when hers was generously refilled.

"Shall I make a toast?" Thomas raised his glass, beaming at Gretchen. She took his hand and raised her glass, happiness radiating on their faces when the girls raised theirs as well. "Today we have our only Granddaughter joining us at our table for the very first time. We have waited a truly long while to have you with us and we couldn't be more pleased. You sit before me with my daughter's eyes making our family feel whole once again, and I thank you for it. To new beginnings!" He clinked glasses with Gretchen and then raised them to Abby, Kieran and Phoebe when they did the same.

Abby took a long sip before setting it down, folding her hands uncomfortably in her lap. Her mind apparently could only think with raging hormones when she was around Kieran and having those thoughts in front of her Grandparents was horribly awkward. She knew the look on her face, that was trying to be polite ease, was more a look of tragic constipation. It was like puberty all over again.

"So how are your parents doing, Kieran? Well, I hope. I had hoped to visit with them when I was traveling but they always seemed a town ahead of me."

"They're well, thank you. They said to pass on a hello."

"Good. Very good to hear." Thomas took Gretchen's hand to his lips and kissed it tenderly. "Abby, my Gretchen says that she had a lovely talk with you today."

"Yes sir, it was a nice chat." *Nice but strange as hell*, Abby thought.

"Wonderful. I'm so sorry that I wasn't here when you arrived. I was, unfortunately kept away on business and you, well - surprised us - with how soon you arrived." He smirked and winked at Kieran. Abby looked at him beside her and he seemed to blush behind a guilty smile.

The smell of garlic and oregano wafted around them when Maggie and two gentlemen Abby had yet to meet arrived with trays of plated pasta. Her stomach rumbled when an enormous plate of spaghetti was placed in front of her. They set about serving each person at the table before refilling wine and placing cloth covered baskets of bread about the table.

Abby whispered to a silent Phoebe next to her, "Did you tell them that spaghetti is my favorite?"

"Nope." Phoebe smiled mischievously, sprinkling cheese across her dish.

"How was the meeting with David?" Kieran tucked his napkin in his lap as he spoke.

"I'd have to say it was productive, actually. It was better than was to be expected. Your father has done well once again, my boy."

"Good to hear. Hopefully he'll have them out of the area sooner rather than later."

Erick raised his glass before taking a sip. "Here, here." He really did seem to be a very warm man. His eyes twinkled when he smiled and he appeared beam when he looked at Abby. Her attention turned to her grandmother, who appeared to be the exact opposite of her grandfather at the moment. Leaning back in her chair, she was glaring at Phoebe. Confused, Abby glanced at Phoebe beside her and found her seemingly completely oblivious to the icy daggers Gretchen was shooting her way.

Thomas leaned towards Gretchen, speaking quietly. Whatever he had said earned him a flash of an angry look before the smile returned to her face and she resumed sipping her wine.

"We are quite proud of how you are handling all that's been thrust at you. You most certainly have your mother's bravery." Thomas regarded Abby for a moment. "I don't want to push you, but I would love to have you remain with us for some time. There are a lot of things I would like you to learn about yourself and your family. I do believe you would be an amazing asset to all of us."

"Now Thomas, she's agreed to stay for a few days. Let her absorb as much as she can without you pressuring her." Gretchen placed her hand on her husband's shoulder, looking up at him with unspoken words.

"Of course, yes. No pressure on you at all, my dear." He gave a quick nod to her before he tucked into his dinner.

They all ate in an uncomfortable silence; Abby was unsure what to say. She wanted to ask about her mother, her life here and if they ever saw her again after she had met her dad but it felt like awkward. She'd been cursed with a million unanswered questions and no clue on how, when or to whom she should ask.

"Are you glad to be done with your studies, ladies?" Thomas' voice pulled them all back to the table.

"I'm super happy, Mr. Ambrose. Mainly because I can sleep in again." Everyone chuckled at Phoebe. "Those early morning classes were rough. Especially since we had to drive an hour each way because this one wouldn't live in the residence." She bumped Abby's arm making her slop her spaghetti back onto her plate.

"And now you'll be joining us again, I expect?"

Phoebe wiped her mouth slowly with her napkin. "Well...I guess I'll go where Abby goes." Her eyes darted between Gretchen and Thomas. "But if she wants to stay and I'm welcome here with her, I'd love to come back."

Gretchen sat forward, considering Phoebe. "You have been a very good friend to our granddaughter, Miss Blake." She looked to a still beaming Thomas before turning back to her. "If Abigail decides to remain here, you are more than welcome to join us as well."

Phoebe's back straightened a touch, her eyes wide. "Thank you, Mrs. Ambrose." She grabbed her wine and took a mouthful before setting it down, turning a happy grin to Abby.

"Um, Mr. Ambrose?"

"Mr. Ambrose? Please, my dear Abby! No need to be so formal. I would presume grand pappy is a bit of a wishful reach but I'd settle for Thomas." His laugh made Abby feel more at ease.

"Ok, sorry, Thomas." Abby could see why everyone spoke so fondly of him. "If I were to stay, and I'm not saying I am, but if I was to stay, what would I do here? Could I come and go as I wanted?"

"Be careful Abby, you might get your sweet old *grand pappy's* hopes up." Gretchen smiled with humor.

She laughed but with some discomfort. Conversation had never been her forte, let alone when the subject could have such weight. "I'm just wondering why you would want me here."

Maggie came around with a tray to collect the dishes with another woman who followed behind with coffee. Kieran, who had been quiet for most of the meal, thanked her politely. Gretchen waited until they had descended down the stairs before answering.

"You're our family, Abby. Our blood and we have missed out on so much of your life with you. We merely want you to spend time with us. To get to know us." Thomas took Gretchen's hand to his lips again, keeping ahold of it when he set it back on the table.

Maggie appeared up the stairs, "Excuse me Mr. and Mrs. Ambrose, so sorry to interrupt, but there's an urgent call waiting in the study. They insist it can not wait."

Thomas sighed heavily, looking to his wife. "I'm terribly sorry, please excuse us everyone." He tossed his napkin on the table and rose. "Abby, I hope we can speak again soon. But unfortunately business calls." He pressed his lips to Gretchen's head. "I will be as fast as I possibly can, love." They shared a loving look that made Abby blush and look away from the intimacy of it. Her grandparents were truly in love. When they looked at each other like they were at that moment, it made her think of her parents and how in love they were. She peeked over at Kieran at the same moment he stole a glance of her. She smiled to herself at the idea she could have what they had.

"I'll join you actually." Gretchen stood from the table. "We have some things that would be best to have addressed soon rather than later."

"Fair point, love. Abby, I apologize again, but I hope this to one of many meals that we all share."

Phoebe stood from the table after they disappeared down the pathway. "Is anyone else freezing? I'm going in to make a tea. Would you two lovebirds care to join me?"

"Phoebe, oh my god." Abby's eyes widened and a blush covered her face, but Kieran just laughed.

"Oh calm down, Abby. Come on." She started back up to the house, Kieran falling in step beside Abby. It had been an awkward dinner mostly, but it was a surreal moment for her. She felt saddened that her grandparents hadn't been with her for so many of life's moments. Taking away the bizarre family business, they appeared to be a grandchild's dreams come true.

Maggie was waiting for them at the door. "Mr. Bernard, the Ambrose's have requested you join them in the study."

"Thank you Maggie. I'm sorry Abby. I have to go too, apparently. I'll catch up with you tomorrow if that's alright?" He kissed her cheek quickly when she nodded. "Have fun girls."

Phoebe waited until he was out of earshot before tugging Abby into the kitchen by her sleeve. "Could you be any more gaga for him? Yowza, Abb's."

"Oh, shush you." Abby leaned against the counter watching her pull out a box of tea and set the kettle on the huge gas range. The kitchen was bright and airy, even at night, with a row of cream cupboards lining a dusty grey granite countertop in between an industrial looking fridge and stove set on one side of a breakfast bar, and a wall of French doors over looking the lake on the other.

"I'm sorry. I know I shouldn't tease you, but it's so sweet to see the way you guys look at each other. It's crazy that he's so connected to you. We've all spent years wondering what would happen after we found out about him. And to see it, how it seems so normal. Well, normal compared to how ever normal Patron's love lives can be. Who would have known?" Phoebe rummaged through the fridge, pulling out milk and a half eaten blueberry pie. "Score!"

"What do you mean it seems so normal?" Every conversation in the past few days just brought up more questions than answers for Abby.

"Just that no one knew what to make of your mom running away to be with your dad, and then *you* came along and no even knew what you were technically. And then Kieran…"

Abby cut her off. "So we're freaks? My mom, me, Kieran, we're freaks to you and everyone here?"

"You're not a freak, Abby." Phoebe laughed. "Don't be so dramatic. You're taking this in pretty well, buttercup. I know I keep saying it but if you came to me and told me I was actually a transient… I would be freaking out – and I already knew those people existed." She pushed a hot cup of tea to Abby when the kettle boiled, pulled forks from a drawer and carried her mug and the pie into the sitting room with the giant TV next to the kitchen. "So you guys are different. Who cares as long as you're happy, right? But you're not a freak. I'm a Banshee that just graduated college alongside people who wouldn't believe what I am in million years." She curled up beside Abby on the couch. "Do you feel it now?"

"Feel what? Being different? Or the bond thing?"

Phoebe pursed her lips at her.

"I don't know, Phoebe, I honestly don't know what to think about it all. How should I know what it feels like?" She pulled her knees up to her chin, and leaned back against the couch. "I mean I like him...a lot, but how do I know it's not just because he's gorgeous and sweet and how do I know it's not just because I'm being told that we're meant to be together and..."

"Abby, slow down." She gave a sympathetic smile, pulling her to her side and Abby tucked her head on her shoulder.

"It's just all so much to take in. I met a Vampire today, for god's sake, and he could go outside in the daytime!"

Phoebe's eyes flashed from a wicked grin. "Ooooh...Did you meet Marcus?" Her eyebrows waggled up and down.

"I did. From the look on your face, I'm guessing you know him?" Abby sat up and pulled a puffy cushion onto her lap.

"Oh, I *know* Marcus." The saucy smile spread across her face and Abby wacked her with the pillow making her explode in giggles. "I know him reeeeeeally well." She scooped up a huge mouthful of pie.

"Seriously? You've slept with a Vampire?" Abby tried to imagine what that would even be like. Would it be different?

"It's actually weirder to me that I've slept with transients, but a girls gotta do who a girl wants to do!" She flicked the TV on to a pop music station and tossed the remote on the table before turning back to Abby, mockingly mirroring the look of surprise on her face. "What? Some of us don't have the stars above casting true love at our feet, so it's a perk I take full advantage of."

"Does...did he bite you?"

"Not the way you're implying! Gross! I'm not his food, Abby."

"Silly me." Abby rolled her eyes and laughed. "What a ridiculous thing to ask, my apologies. But what about delectable David, your bartender love?"

Her breath shot quickly in a single chuckle. "Delectable David, nice." She looked at her nails, picking at a chip of nail polish. "I really need to get my nails done."

"Don't change the subject, Phoebe. You know you like him." For someone who kept some pretty huge secrets, Phoebe was sometimes terrible at diverting attention from subjects she wanted to avoid.

"Ok, he doesn't bite me either. Yet."

"Pheebs, come on be serious!"

"Well that doesn't matter anymore so let's move on." The tension in her voice was quick but very real. "You're just so love struck now, you think we all are. So what did you think of Marcus? Hot, right?"

"He *was* pretty cute. But I'm sure I made an ass of myself. I froze when I saw his teeth!" Abby buried her face in her hands. "And how can he even go out in the sun? Is there any truth to the stories about all of them?"

"All of *us*, sweetie. You and me both are a part of that too. And it's like any other folklore. The truth becomes a little more and a little less to suit the story."

Abby considered that for a moment. The idea that she was a part of a secret society of what she had always considered to be fictional ghouls. It was beyond just having a family that had been hidden from her; it was a whole world that she was a part of. It wasn't just a secret she had been let in on, but she herself was one of the ghouls.

"Why didn't you want to tell me?" Abby set her cup down and tucked her legs up, facing Phoebe.

"Tell you what?" Phoebe spoke around another mouthful of pie.

"You know exactly what. All of this. About me, about you." She seemed pretty happy there, and the perks were obvious, but there had to be a reason why she was so upset when Kieran came into her world.

"Because I'm a selfish bitch." Phoebe set the pie plate on the table, sadness in her voice. "And I am really sorry, Abbs."

"What is that supposed to mean? You've never been anything but the best friend I've ever had. How could you protecting me from something so bizarre make you a bitch?" She couldn't understand the melancholy in her friend's voice.

"I didn't tell you because I was living a different life before I came here and I was really loving just living a life without the responsibilities of here. Without…everything that I am here." Her eyes started to mist up, looking anywhere but Abby. "I thought that if you didn't know about it, it wouldn't matter. I didn't think… I just didn't think, and now I have a lot of apologies to make. But that's for another time." She wiped her eye quickly with the back of her hand before pressing a tight smile on her face. "Next question?"

Maggie's voice startled them when she walked into the room. "I'm terribly sorry to interrupt, but Mr. Ambrose has requested you join him in the study, Miss. Blake."

"Why am I starting to get the feeling this little meeting tonight has been about me?" Abby watched her down the rest of her tea and stand to leave.

"Don't worry, it's probably nothing. You stay here long enough and they'll start having a million jobs for you too. I don't know how long I'll be so I'll probably just see you tomorrow, ok?" Maggie trailed behind Phoebe out of the room and down the hall out of sight.

Abby decided to turn in for the night, and making her way to the stairs she wondered what it would be like to live here, like this, all the time. Would she still be able to work in a museum? It had been her dream for so long and she had dedicated herself to doing well in school, it would be horrible to just give that all up to do who knows what here. She passed a few people in the foyer, who smiled politely and carried on their way. She wondered if they were some of the other natured people because they didn't look any different than people she would pass on the street. What she did find strange was how people seemed to come and go there as if it were a hotel. It certainly wasn't a cozy home at all, and she couldn't picture strangers walking up and down the hall of her home. That's one of the main reasons she didn't want to live in the dormitories, even though Phoebe begged her to. Privacy was very important to her and that seemed to be another thing she was about to lose.

Her thoughts turned to her Aunt and Uncle when she crawled in bed, hoping to be able to see them soon and hoping that they can still be a part of her life as they had been. She worried, though, remembering her Grandmother saying they would be in danger if they knew about her, and about what she knew now. *Who would hurt them?* As she drifted off to sleep her mind filled with her mother's voice calling her further into the woods, the shadow trying to pull her down to the forest ground and she chased her through her dreams until morning.

# Chapter 7

She woke up tired, but the sun beaming through the windows wouldn't let her sleep any longer. After a warm, lingering shower she found her way back down to the kitchen. Phoebe was perched on a stool at the long breakfast bar, flipping through a magazine and inhaling a bowl of cereal.

"Morning buttercup! Good sleep?" She patted the stool next to her and slid a mug over. The smell of coffee perked her up and she yawned, joining Phoebe at the counter.

"Not the greatest. Dreams kept me tossing and turning all night." She stirred her cup before taking a sip.

"Ooooh tossing and turning on Kieran kinda dream?" She refilled her mug, shoveling in spoonfuls of sugar, while Abby rolled her eyes at her continually frisky friend. "Oh please. Sometimes the heat on your cheeks speaks to the heat you want in your sheets."

"Not at all. My mom again." Abby rubbed at a headache that was trying to take root. "In the forest again."

"The forest? Oh. I'm sorry, sweetie. You've had a quite a lot happen in the last few days. Nightmares are to be expected I'd think." She slung an arm over her in a quick hug. "Are you good on your own for the day? I hate to leave you but I have some stuff I have to take care of."

"Sure, I'm good. Is everything ok?" Her voice had an edge to it that made Abby feel she wasn't talking about errands.

"Of course, everything's fine, I just need to look after some things." She flashed a bright smile.

"Ok." Abby blew into her coffee before taking another sip. "Is it Banshee business?"

Phoebe snorted into her cup. "Banshee business?" Her eyes danced with humor. "No, I don't have 'Banshee Business', dork. It's non-Banshee related. Namely an afternoon of cocktails with a gentleman caller." She winked and hopped off of the stool. "I'll find you when I get back, ok?" She gave Abby a peck on the cheek and bounced out of the room, passing Kieran who was on his way in and gave her a nod. He opened the fridge, grabbing a carton of orange juice and then a tall glass from the cupboard before sliding onto the stool Phoebe had just left.

"She's got a bounce in her step this morning, doesn't she? What's his name?" He snickered, pouring his juice.

"She didn't give me a name, but did say it was a gentleman." she smiled as she gulped her coffee, feeling more awake.

"A gentleman? Well then. So does that mean I have you all to myself today?" He tucked a lock of her hair behind her ear, his lips turned up into a shy grin.

"It looks like you do." She raised her hand to her lips in an attempt to hide the delight that was creeping onto her face. "What do you have in mind?"

He stood up, draining the last of his glass. "Follow me, I want to show you something." He stretched out his hand, taking hers as she stepped down from the seat. Standing this near to him she noticed how much taller he really was than her, her head coming only to his shoulder. He linked their fingers, opening one of the French doors with his free hand, and led them out into the warm morning sunshine. A path that led around the side of the house turned into a well-worn dirt trail that made its way into the lush forest of pine trees, that seemed a mile high, and they followed along in silence, Kieran's hand behind his back locked on hers. Being in the woods brought her right back to the dreams she'd been having of her mom; the evergreen's crisp smells, the blackbirds chirping in the trees, everything was just as real now as when she was sleeping. Without the cold shadows that clung to her ankles, pulling her to the ground of course. A clearing appeared with a small log cabin in the center. With shuttered windows on either side of a bright red door and a stone chimney on the side, it was right out of fairytale.

"It's so lovely!" Abby let go of Kieran's hand to run ahead to it. "All it needs is a little bluebird perched on the window sill!"

Kieran was beaming at her reaction when he walked up and opened the door. "This was your mother's."

She tried the door handle and when it opened to the cabin with a squeak she poked her head inside, taking in the rustic décor.

An old cast-iron stove sat in the far corner beside an icebox, a pine dining set in front that matched a pine log couch and chair, with quilts tossed over them, in front of the stone fireplace. Abby recognized the pieced quilts right away to be the ones her mother loved to make, with every color of the rainbow exploding on them. The opposite wall had a matching set of bunk beds with more of the quilts and a large cupboard with painted flowers carved up the door.

"She lived here?" She tried to picture her mother living like Snow White in the woods, the idea of it giving her a laugh. They stepped inside and the musty smell of being unused lingered in the air.

"No she didn't live here, this was just her special place. She'd come here when she wanted to be alone. Erick had it built for her for her thirteenth birthday. He said she spent a lot of time in here."

"This was her fort?" Abby laughed out loud at that. No matter how extravagant the Manor was, the idea that this was her mother's playhouse was unbelievable. It was a fully functioning home in the woods. Her mother took great pride in the blanket forts they would make when Abby was small, as if they had built their own kingdom in the TV room. There wasn't even a shadow of an idea that she came from this.

"You could say that, ya. It's been more of a shrine to you her, and you, for a very long time now." He walked to the cupboard, "Look inside." He gestured towards the intricate door with a nod of his head and a smile. Abby swung the doors open to reveal small shelves from top to bottom packed with trinkets. A small silver jewelry box, beside a dusty old bird's nest that sat beside a pile of shiny rocks filled one shelf. Another shelf was lined with dried flowers and leaves. Every shelf was filled with random little items and her eyes stopped on a wooden plaque, centered on the top shelf, with 'Lucy's Cabinet of Curiosities' painted in bright blue paint. She reached up and traced her fingers along the letters, her heart swelling with the images of her mom that were flashing through her mind. Every time they'd go into the woods she would come out with pockets filled with little bits just like this entire cupboard was filled with. It's where her love of collecting and preserving the unique had its heart. She tried to wipe away the glaze that had started to blur her vision. She wasn't so much sad as touched to see a piece of how her mom was when she was here and to know she kept that spirit with her until the day she passed.

"This is so my mom – all of this – is so much my mom." She closed the door, wiping her eyes on the back of her sleeve. "I can't believe this was her version of a fort in the forest though." Abby chuckled at the posh playhouse.

"Phoebe and I used to hang out here a lot when I first got here." They sat down on the couch and looked around at the cabin. There wasn't a dust sprinkling that you would expect of a hidden cottage in the woods. It was clearly still cared for after her mother had left so many years before. She pictured Phoebe when she was an adorable little girl with her bursts of flame red hair sticking out the sides of her head in pigtails. She could see her running around the woods, but the thought of a tiny version of Kieran alongside her made her smile. She could picture his big blue eyes set on a sweet little face, chasing a bossy little Phoebe around this cabin. Living in a world she didn't even know existed, and having the time of their lives.

"When did you get here? Did your parents live here too?"

"I was twelve years old when I came here with my parents. And they stayed here until a few years ago when they went back out east to where we're from."

"Do you miss them? Like, your family and your home?" Abby could relate because she was already missing her aunt and uncle desperately, and it had only been a few days.

"I do. Sometimes I do, for sure, but they're only a call or Skype away. I'm much better here and they're where they're needed." He leaned his head back on the back of the couch; his head turned to Abby and took her hand. "I've been lucky to have found a place alongside Erick while I've been here. It's filled my time and given me meaning to my life that I needed. A focus, I guess. I like being able to make a difference." He rested his eyes on her gently. "It gave me something else to think about."

"Am I the reason you're here? I mean, am I the reason you and your family came here?" The idea seemed ridiculous but her heart slipped into her stomach with the way he was regarding her.

"You are." He watched his fingers trace along her jaw.

"How do you really know that I'm supposed to be the one? I mean, how do you *know*?" She had yet to have anyone tell her what she was supposed to be feeling. Not that she had much of any time to really think about any of this. She did have to admit that she felt closer to him than she had with any other guy, and so quickly. And for being so uncomfortable around other people in the past, he certainly made her feel at ease. But from what she had taken away from what these people were, they had a pretty singular idea of love.

He moved his arm to the back of the couch, his eyes moving to the window beside the old fireplace. He pursed his lips as he pondered the question. "I don't know how to describe that to you." He shifted on the couch to face her. "It's sort of like how I know water is wet, or fire is hot. I don't remember the first time I felt either one of those but I'll always know the feeling of both. Does that make any sense?"

"Not at all." She laughed when Kieran did, covering his face with his hand.

"Well, let's start from the beginning when I dreamed of you."

"You dreamed of me? Before we met?" Abby was trying to stop her face from showing how weirded out that sounded to her. The crooked grin he gave told that she wasn't hiding it very well.

"I did, but not in a perverted way, don't worry." He leveled his eyes to hers and she noticed he had actual flecks of metallic blue in his irises that glimmered in the light. The effect was startling. "That's how it starts for us. I saw your face and this town and your mother; and when I first saw you in my first dream I knew what it felt like to love you. And I've felt the same way ever since."

Abby's mouth was dry when she tried to respond, the heat spreading up her chest and to her cheeks. He spoke so easily about such deep feelings. He was so sure in his words and the way he looked at her every single time told her that he meant it. "But how did you know it was me? How did you know how to find me?"

"You told me your name." His crooked smile deepened.

"I told you my name." She meant it as a question but it just fell as a statement between them.

"That's how it works. Easy peasy." He chuckled lightly, kissing her hand. He turned her hand over to place a melting kiss on her palm before sliding his fingers between hers, her hand feeling shaky now. "But you, my dear, were a real quandary for all of us because we didn't know how you would react - with your dad being...you know, different." His eyes narrowed when he pressed a grimaced smile. "I don't mean that to be rude, it's just no one was sure about what that would change in you...or how you'd react...because of being... you know, half...different." He drew her hand up to his lips again, looking away from her. "We didn't know if you would have the same reaction to me... or if you'd have any feelings at all. They didn't know what to do with me as long as they didn't know what to do with you." Abby's eyes felt frozen on his, while the rest of her body burned. "Do you feel...different for me? Different from what you've felt...romantically, before?" His voice was soft and unsure, his fingers nervously grazing hers.

At that moment she realized that she really did care more for him than other guy before, even though she barely knew him. She thought it could be the intensity of his feelings clouding her own or maybe she really did feel that deeply towards him; either way she couldn't explain the fact that she was falling in love with a virtual stranger.

"I do." Kieran's body went rigged, as if he were to move she would run away. "I do feel... different." She leaned forward and lightly pressed her lips to his. "I can't explain it but I do." He flashed a look of disbelief before relief when what she said met his lips. And then the most dazzling smile lit up his face. His mouth slammed into hers, his hands sliding up into her hair sending bursts of fire through every nerve in her body. His kiss softening, he wrapped an arm around her waist, pulling her against him until she felt the warmth of his chest press against her. Abby's hands trailed up the lean muscles in his back until he broke from her lips to graze tiny kisses across her face. Hands cupping her face gently, he cocked his head to the side, his smiling lighting up his face.

"Abby... I..." He shook his head, trying to find the words he was searching for. "We all knew you were exceptional before any of us had met you. You are like nothing we've ever seen before, but you are impossibly more than that. You are extraordinary." There had to be something in her that came from her mother's blood because she'd never felt like this before about anyone. Being this close to Kieran made it hard to think and she had to sit back against the arm of the couch to take a breath. This in itself was extraordinary and impossible to explain.

"I'm sorry, I don't mean to make you feel smothered but I've just waited so long to be...near you." He sat back from her, his arms crossed against his chest. "This is new for me too. I've never needed to learn boundaries before." His face squeezed at his words. "Wow that sounded super creepy. I'm so sorry." An uncomfortable laugh shook his chest as he stared at the floor, his elbows on his knees.

"No it's fine really, I swear." She waited until he looked up at her so she could give him a reassuring smile. "This is strange for both of us and that is the most comforting thing I have going for me right now. I've spent the last few days feeling like I was a freak of nature in two different worlds so I love that you're as strange as me in all off of this. It's nice to have a comrade."

His eyes glistened when his lips twitched up. "So you and me are me and you in a pretty strange way. I'm good with that." He rubbed his face up and down with his hands and stood up. "Ok, so let's ease into this. How about I show you around some more before Phoebe comes to squirrel you away again?" She took his outstretched hand and let him pull her up from the couch.

"That sounds good to me." Abby was interested to see the rest of the manor and the surrounding grounds, but she was also looking forward to spending time with Kieran. Doing something that could distract her from the fact that all she could think about was having their hands all over each other. If she was going to spend time trying to understand any of this previously secret world like her Grandmother had asked she'd have to keep her wits about her, and her pants on. So far the only thing that could make her forget how soft his lips are, how he smells like warm citrus soap and the way his stare tears through her to all the right places, was the chance to learn about her mom, and how she grew up with this family she knew so little about. Everywhere she had looked in the last few days she had tried to see her mother living her life here, feeling as out of place as she now did. She was always an amazing person in Abby's eyes when she was a little girl. Lucy Ambrose was her hero. She glowed like the glamorous women that she had looked at in her mom's glossy magazines, even when she was down playing in the dirt with her. But the fact that she had been this whole other person, knowing about all of this – not knowing what would come of Abby being a part of her from all of this – and she dealt with it all to be with her dad - the wonderful, larger than life Adam Whitmore - made her the most unbelievably incredible woman to her.

They made their way from the cottage hand in hand in a haze. It slammed into her how ridiculously unreal her mother should seem to her, even with the glossing effect time had on people we lose. She was even more than she even imagined, and her love for her father seemed so much deeper. It was against everything they were to be together and they proved them wrong. If she were to ever put into words what pure love was, it was her parents. Lucy and Adam Whitmore loved each other in a way that no one could look away from. Even when they fought, it was with a mischievous glimmer in their eye that showed they appreciated the challenge, and loved each other more for what they were on their own. Together they made a link that stood against everything. Looking up at the manor, as it appeared through the trees at the end of the trail, she tried to imagine her beautiful mother as a little girl running towards the forest, her pale blond hair bouncing around her. She wondered if her father had been here, how they had met. She had never questioned how she didn't have an extended family, a lot of the kids that she grew up with didn't. How could she possibly imagine that her family extended past any reality she knew? She had worked so hard to try and establish herself in a world that had made her feel so lost when she lost her parents, and now she was given a world that was beyond anything she knew to be real.

They walked up the stone steps to the porch and Kieran opened the door before stepping aside for her to pass through, a devilish grin covering his face. "I have to get something from my room so wait right here. Don't move in inch."

Abby matched his smile watching him hop two stairs at a time and sat down on one of the giant wing chairs that Phoebe had been splayed across the day before. She smiled to herself at how much a life could change in a moment. Her biggest moment in her life, graduating college, was just a few days ago. She had worked so hard for it, and it was something that meant so much to her. Seeing her mother's dusty old collections in the cabin reminded her how much of her love of museums was linked to her and that she was doing it in part to keep her mother's memory alive in her heart. But just like that, the world she thought she was living in shifted and everything changed. And it now included more of her mother than she had lived with in years. She pictured the world she had worked so hard to make her place in, alongside the fantastic world she'd been shown in such a short time. She looked around the impressive main hall of the home her mother was born into and felt like it was a dream. She's only pictured people living like this in magazines and over the top reality TV. Muffled voices coming from down the hall caught her attention when she heard her name. Frozen in her seat, she listened to her Grandfather's distinct voice.

"Abby's being here is a blessing, don't you understand that? There is no question about it. She cannot be anywhere else now. Not safely. Not anymore." A woman's voice she didn't know spoke words she couldn't make out before Thomas' voice boomed. "If we had known that Alastair's actions would have taken my Lucy from me, I would have intervened! It was deplorable enough what he did to Adam, but my little girl was taken from me because we didn't protect her! When he took Adam's life, he stole my baby girl forever. I will not lose Abby, as well. You can be god damn certain that I will intervene this time."

Abby's heart stopped at his words, every inch of her started to shake when the words ran over and over in her head. Nausea folded through her stomach, bile rising up in her throat, until all she could think was that her daddy had died in an accident. She was always told it was an accident. Everything seemed to spin until Kieran's face was in front of her.

"Abby, what's wrong? What's happened?" His face was almost nose-to-nose with her trying to shake her from her terrified thoughts. She got up from the chair, pulling herself from his arms and walked towards the door.

"Who's Alastair?" her voice was unsteady and louder than she intended.

"What?" Kieran tried to take her hand and she pulled away again.

"Who is Alastair, Kieran?" She shouted the words.

"Alastair? You mean Phoebe's father?" Her heart pounded as a chill crawled from her face to her toes. Feeling like she was going to pass out she grabbed the door handle, twisting it blindly before it clicked open, and stepped on the porch. She turned to look back at Kieran to see Thomas hurrying towards the foyer, a look of horror on his face when he saw her and a woman with blazing red hair following closely.

"Abby, please, let me explain." Thomas pleaded to her as he rushed to the door.

She ignored him and turned her attention to Kieran. "Take me home." He started to argue before she cut him off. "Take me home, now." She turned and started walking when he just stared at her, his face pained with confusion. "You people killed my dad! You *are* monsters!" Her feet carried her up the driveway as her eyes flooded with tears. Her mind spun as everything that had happened, everything that she'd been told slammed into her all at once. The idea that her parents were killed because of whatever freak of nature she was stained her mind. There was no accident. There was probably no cancer, either. It had to be because of what a mistake she was, a mistake she didn't know she was until a few days ago. Phoebe was her best friend in the whole world, practically her sister, and her father was the one that took her parents away from her forever. She turned onto the road that led around the lake and started to run. She needed to be home, she needed everything to go back as it was. She had given Gretchen the few days, as she'd asked, and now Abby was done with it all. For all she knew they were deranged psychopaths and that's why her mom had left them in the first place and never looked back – it certainly made a lot more sense than anything they had told her. It would certainly explain why Phoebe never wanted to talk about her parents. A car's horn behind her made her scramble to the side of the road. Kieran screeched an older looking silver car to a stop beside her, throwing open the door and grabbed her arm when she tried to keep walking.

"Abby, please! Stop, talk to me." He was out of breath when he spoke and planted his feet in the dirt covering the shoulder of the road, stopping Abby in place. She spun around and pulled her arm from him to drag the tears from her face with the back of her hand. "Abby, please." His voice was calmer, quieter. "I didn't know. I swear I didn't know." Her eyes were blurred with the silent tears that poured down her face.

"That doesn't change how fucked up all of this is, Kieran." She turned her back to him to start up the road again, but he kept pace, leaving his car running with the door gaped open. "Just leave me alone. I'm serious."

"Don't do this, Abby, please. Come back and talk to Erick, he's beside himself. I don't understand exactly what's going on, but just come back with me. Let him explain."

She was pained when she took a sideways glance at him, not breaking her pace. He was locked on her, his face washed in concern when he stepped forward to stop her, his hands on her shoulders.

"I can't, I'm sorry. I need to be alone. My entire world has been turned upside down and pissed on and I just need to be alone. Please, Kieran, I need to be away from…" She looked back in the direction of the manor "…whatever *that* is." Turning back to Kieran, he dropped his hands from her looking defeated. "I need to be alone right now, ok?" She wanted to slap him, for being one of them, for being a part of such a catastrophic disaster her life had become, but instead reached up and pressed her lips lightly on his cheek. He closed his eyes, leaning into her.

"Ok." His voice was only a whisper.

She started back up the road, not looking back. She wanted to go straight to Aunt Julie and Uncle Thomas but her face was ruddy and puffed from crying would only lead to questions she didn't know how to answer. She found herself heading down the trail to the cemetery that held her parents. There weren't any answers to be found there, but she just needed to be near them. Sitting on the grass between their headstones, picking at the flowers that had withered since she left them the week before, she felt the tears start again and buried her face in her hands. Everything she knew about her parents was a lie. The weight of everything that had happened poured down on her. It was hard enough to be told of a secret world that her secret family lived in, but now memories of her parents streamed as quickly as her sobs. Her dad gingerly twirling her mom around the living room, dancing to their favorite songs, her mom rushing to the hall mirror to fuss with her hair and straighten her clothes when she heard his car coming up the driveway, the way they would sit in contented silence on the porch, her dad holding her hand to him. Faded memories that were cut short years ago. And now an entirely new family has appeared and in three days they have made her question every moment she's saved of her parents in her mind. Reaching up to trace her fingers along the engraved names on the granite, she had never missed her them as much as she did at that moment.

"My condolences." The words startled her from her thoughts and she realized she had been sitting there long enough for the sun to start setting. She looked up behind her to find eyes almost black regarding her. "I didn't mean to frighten you, my dear." He was motionless, the hood of his black sweatshirt covering his head. Abby scrambled to her feet, becoming aware that she was about to be in a dark cemetery with this creepy stranger.

"Um…thank you." She turned to head back up the path, trying to act unnerved.

"It's a terrible thing to lose your parents, isn't it?" His voice made her blood run cold and she froze. "I'm assuming they *were* your parents, of course." She turned slowly back to him to find him sitting on her father's headstone.

"They *are* my parents, yes. And I'd appreciate it if you didn't disrespect them. Please get off of there." She steeled herself against the slithering smile that crawled across his face.

"My, my, you turned out to be a strong woman…for an orphan. You must be a very special young lady." He hopped off of the stone but didn't take a step forward. Her stomach clenched at his words but her voice didn't waver.

"They were very special parents." His eyes narrowed when she spoke, her voice strong.

"So I've heard." His pale tongue traced the corner of his lips.

"Michael, I believe you were just leaving."

Abby spun around to find Kieran standing at the head of the trail, the fury on his face coming off of him in waves. His glare went straight past her to the frightening man on the other side of her. "Now."

"Oh my, my, my. Lover to the rescue, how endearing." His eyes we're locked on Kieran defiantly but he slowly moved behind the headstone as he spoke. "We're just having a chat, handsome. Nothing that need involve you."

"I'm not saying it again, you piece of shit." Kieran moved quickly towards him, making the stranger stumble back from the graves, but he stopped at Abby's side and slid her behind him. "Go."

"I was just leaving, bossy boy." He sneered at Kieran and then turned back to Abby. "I just wanted to pay my respects, of course." She felt Kieran tense when the creepy hooded man turned and skulked away into the trees along the cemetery. As soon he was out of sight Kieran spun around and gripped her arms. He looked her over as if she'd been struck by lightening.

"Are you ok? Did he lay a finger on you?" He blew a relieved breath when he didn't find any injury or marks on her and pulled her to his chest.

"Who the hell was that?" Abby noticed she was shivering in his arms from the chill of the night air and the burst of adrenalin that had overtaken her.

"No one that matters, just someone to stay away from." He pressed his lips onto the top of her head and held her out to look her over again.

"I'm fine, Kieran, honestly." She backed away from him, looking up the path to make sure the creep was gone. "How did you even know I was here? Did you follow me?"

He bent his knees down so they were eye to eye, but she couldn't read the emotions clouding his face, emotions that he was trying to find the words for.

"I'll always find you, Abby. I will always find you." His face was clearly showed pain after he spoke.

"I need to go home. Kieran, I've had enough of all of this. I need to go home."

"At least let me drive you." She looked off at the trail, wishing she were already home, waking up from this nightmare, the fatigue of the day overcoming her. "It's dark, Abby, just let me take you home." He smiled so sweetly she couldn't resist him.

"Ok, alright. Thank you." He awkwardly gestured for her to head to the trail, a shy grin and his hand on the small of her back. She shook her head and took his hand. "Come on."

"Who was that, really, Kieran?" Abby nerves were on edge; sure he would pop out of the woods at any moment.

"A nightmare, that's who," Kieran's voice was still angry. "He's someone who's been told to stay away from you." He lightly tugged her arm to turn her to him. "I know you're overwhelmed, and I know you're upset, but he's seriously dangerous."

"So..." She felt the chill return, crawling up her back, at the thought of the creepy man. "What is he? I mean, he's not...normal, right?"

"He's a Crusnik. He's a vampire, Abby." She thought of Marcus and how friendly and handsome he was. Michael on the other hand looked like he was rotting from the inside out. "They feed on other vampires and want nothing more than to destroy everything around them. They're pure twisted evil, Abby. You have to promise to stay away from him."

"You don't have to tell me twice. That guy's creepy as hell."

Kieran took her hand again, heading back up the trail. "And straight from there, as well."

His car was parked at the top of the trail and he moved around to the passenger side to open the door. She sat down into the crimson seat and he closed the door before walking around to slide in behind the wheel. Abby looked over at him as he pulled out onto the street, looking back and forth between the mirrors. His head almost touched to low convertible roof. He caught her looking at him and smirked playfully.

"What?" He looked back and forth from the road and her.

"Why do you have such an old car? You barely fit in it." He looked at her like she had two heads, laughing. "I'm serious! I assumed from what I saw at the manor you would have a fancy car." He laughed again.

"This is a 1957 Porsche 357. She's my baby!" The horror on his face made her laugh.

"Ok, I'm sorry, I'm sorry!" She held her hands up in defeat. "I'm not a car girl."

"Apparently!" He looked gorgeous the way his face lit up with humor. "This was my dad's car and I had to beg him for it for years!" She smiled picturing that; before the memory of the day tensed her again. She chewed at her lip when she silently stared out the window. He reached over, picking up her hand and twining their fingers, and put their hands together on the stick shift. The anger drained from her even though she fought to hold onto it. There was something comforting about being so close to him and no matter how messed up the last few days were, it felt good. They drove along like that until they pulled up to her house.

"Thanks for the ride."

"You're very welcome." He let go of her hand and turned to her.

She didn't know what else to say, until she looked up at the house. "Kieran, how did you know where I live?"

His hand traced his lips and his face became serious. "Abby..." He took a deep breath. "We can't pretend all of this isn't real. You are a very important person in a world you know nothing about. Just because you didn't know about us, doesn't mean we didn't know about you."

"So you've all been stalking me?" The sweet moment they had shared was gone as quickly as it came.

"It's not like that at all. Abby..." The frustration in his voice was very apparent.

"Let's not do this, ok? I just want to go home. And I just want to be with my family and crawl into my bed and just take a break from all of this, ok?" She didn't want to fight with him. All that had happened, all the heartbreak she had felt today, just being with him made her feel better. But she wanted to step away from it all and be able to think on her own. Without his eyes on her, without the foggy way her thoughts became when he was around her and, most definitely, without goblins and vampires and banshees.

"Take your time. I'm here for you when you need me."

She leaned over and kissed him. Just a quick peck but they seemed to linger just outside of it for a moment before she sat back to look at him. No matter what all of this craziness was doing to her, she couldn't resist him. "Thank you."

"Be careful, ok?" She couldn't ignore the seriousness in his voice.

"I will, I just need some space. I just want my own bed, in my own home." She climbed out of the car and walked around to the sidewalk. "Phoebe has my number if you need me." His sad eyes betrayed the tender smile he was giving her. When he could finally drag his eyes away, he gave a quick nod before pulling away and down the street. She watched until he turned the corner and disappeared. Everything seemed so much easier when she thought about him, which was why she needed to process things outside of his orbit. Opening the screen door she wandered into the kitchen looking for her family. Uncle Thomas was spread out on the couch with his laptop on his stomach and his reading glasses perched on his nose.

"Well there's our big city girl! How was it? Any luck?" She forgot she was supposed to be apartment hunting.

"A few promising spots, maybe." She hated lying to him.

He pulled his glasses off and looked at her. "The city was good to you, Sunshine. You look...different." His eyes squinted at her, "Different but good. You're growing up on us, Abby." He turned back to his computer and the TV flashing a PBS NOVA show he always had PVR'd.

"Is that my girl? When did you get home?" Aunt Julie came through the basement door with a laundry basket on her hip. She heaved it onto the kitchen counter before coming to pull Abby into her arms. "We missed you! How was it?" She pushed back to arms length looking her over, as if she could have been wounded or starved in the few days she'd been away from her. Little did she know all of the damage that she couldn't see that was stirring inside of her. Julie's eyes stopped at Abby's with a look of almost awe. "Did you do something new with your makeup?"

"Uh...nope. Just mascara."

Julie stared at her; a small smile traced her lips. "You look so much like your mother right now...I don't know what it is..." She blinked her eyes away. "I must have just missed your face, pretty girl." She kissed Abby's forehead and started to fold the clothes in the basket.

"I'm gonna have a shower before bed, it's been a long day." She was overwhelmed at how good it felt to be home and just wanted to curl up in her bed.

"Ok, sweetie, we'll see you in the morning." She put down the shirt she was folding to beam her happy face at her niece. "I'm so glad you're home. I want all the details on the spots you checked out, missy!"

"Me too, Aunt Julie. I'll see you in the morning. Night Uncle Thomas."

Julie, still beaming, smiled at her and Uncle Thomas waved backwards to her from his laptop, as if she really had just spent a couple of nights in the city. Not the life changing adventure she had been through. She headed upstairs feeling at home again, thinking if only she could forget everything she'd learned. So little time could change everything she knew about the world. She walked into her room, looking around at the normal it held. Everything was in its place. She sat on the bed, dragging her palm across her forehead and lay back on her familiar bed, pulling the pillow over her face. Being at home, in the home that she knew, with the things that that she knew made her feel better. Reaching for her quilt at the end of the bed she patted around until she realized it wasn't there. Her eyes sprung open and she leaned over the side of the bed and then the other before sitting up and looking around the room. The one thing she needed right now was the quilt her mom had made her when she was little and she wasn't going to be able to do any serious thinking without it around her.

Abby wandered downstairs again in search of the blanket and a cup of tea. She made it to the bottom of the stairs when her stomach reminded her that she hadn't eaten all day. Thomas was still settled on the couch, his attention going from his favourite fishing website to the TV still showing the NOVA episode about sunken ships. She filled the kettle and set it on the burner. Staring into the fridge at the options, not wanting to have to actually cook or heat anything up, she pulled out a bowl of chopped watermelon and settled on the arm of the couch to watch the crane on TV try to flip the enormous ship from on its side. Thomas smiled up at her and scooped some melon from the bowl, turning back to his laptop. This was the life that made sense, peaceful and loving, her family being the family she had known all her life. She left the bowl beside him when the kettle whistled.

"Do you want a cup?" She asked knowing that he would.

"Thanks sunshine." He picked up the bowl and popped a piece of melon in his mouth. Abby grabbed her 'You can't be Sirius' mug that Julie got her for her Harry Potter themed birthday party years ago and tossed in a peppermint tea bag. Pulling down Thomas' chipped green mug she dropped in an earl grey.

"Uncle Thomas, have you seen my quilt?" She poured in the boiling water, the minty smell filling the room.

"I think I saw Julie put it on the line earlier. She's been laundry crazy with the nice weather."

That sounded about right. As soon as the spring weather started to turn to summer weather she washed anything fabric that would fit on the clothesline. Julie loved the smell of the sunshine in the house. She pulled the teabags from the cups and tossed them in the garbage and passed Thomas his tea on the way to the back door. She stepped out into the chill of the night and walked across the deck. The motion sensor light didn't light all the way to the end of the line that stretched the long yard, so she hopped down onto the lawn to find her blanket. The moonlight lit up the tall trees in the yard and splashed a line of emerald grass that she followed. Just as he'd said, every blanket in the house was hung out. Her quilt was almost at the end and she couldn't wait it to wrap it around her and snuggle up with the peppermint tea.

"Well hello there, Orphan." She spun around to meet eyes that were as black as nightmares when an icy hand tightened around her neck.

Chapter 8

Abby slowly became aware of the pain that was streaking up her arms into numb fingers when she tried to move into a more comfortable position. Her eyes burst open, catching her breath in her throat, when the burning in her arm cracked into her shoulder. Looking up she saw her arms bound in dirty old rope above that was tied to a metal loop fixed to the wall behind her. She was pulled high enough that she was barely flat-footed and the pain seared through her body.

"Well, the prodigal child has awoken! How are you feeling, Orphan?" She squinted her blurry eyes to see the disturbed man from the cemetery.

"I feel like I'm sick and tired of being knocked the fuck out! That's how I'm feeling." The anger building in her made her more focused on the surroundings. They were in some sort of old shed; the smells of mold and bonfire filling the air. Michael was leaning against the wall opposite her, a slither of a smile twitching on his lips. The only light in the room was a filthy bare light bulb that barely cast a beam, hanging from a cord in the center of the room.

"My goodness, you are right about her, Michael." Another voice, tinged with a Spanish accent, popped from a darkened corner and snapped Abby's attention, her heart starting to thump. "Pretty kitty has a bite!" As he made his way towards her she could see he had the same dead eyes, his grey skin was flat and lifeless in the hazy light. Licking his lips when he stopped a foot from her, he flashed a terrifyingly yellow smile that showed stained fangs – two on each side – and sharp as razors.

"Now, now, Luis. Let's not frighten her too much – my appetite can't be controlled when I hear her delicious heart pounding like that." Michael moved beside him so smoothly it seemed as if he were floating and locked his gaze on Abby. "I haven't decided if she's worth more dead or alive, yet." The smell of rot and mold radiated from them, gagging her.

"But what harm would a little taste do until you decide?" Luis trailed a long, ridged nail down the side of her face to her neck making her strain back against the pain that was now shooting down her back.

"Because you fools have no idea what will happen if you do, so shush." A woman with thick long hair as dark as ink walked in through a creaking crooked door. She was easily a head taller than the two cretins that were crawling around in front of Abby. "And you best back away before you make all of this pointless." She slinked up to Abby with the curves in motion of Marilyn Monroe, her hazel eyes looking her up and down, before turning to face the creeps. "Now back the hell up, you repulsive corpses." She moved them back from her with a flick of her wrist as she regarded her as if she were an expensive purchase. "So this… is Abby."

Abby wanted to get as far away from them as she could, but even with her terror immobilizing her, the pain ripping through her shoulders wouldn't let her move. "What do you want with me?" Her body began to tremble intensely when she spoke.

"You're here, my darling, because *you* are of *value*." Her face curled into a puckish sneer, her eyes burning into Abby's, making the room suddenly feel smaller and more dangerous. She could feel her heart beat shaking her bones when she looked back and forth between the three psychopaths sizing her up. She knew if there was ever a time to not show fear, this was it. She tensed her jaw against the pain and willed herself not to cry, focusing on her anger instead.

"How am I of value to you? I don't know much about any of this but I'm pretty sure I'm the black sheep of your twisted ass world. I'm the outcast. I'm worthless." She forced her chin up defiantly, fighting through the burning ache she felt from every twitch of her body.

"Oh you're worth a hell of a lot, Orphan." Michael snaked around the authoritative woman. "I've never developed a taste for the fragile humans but with that splash of Patron that I can see in your eyes, swimming around inside of you, you could be a delectable treat." The disgusting smell of him filled Abby's nose the closer he got, a mixture of rotten meat and wet dirt, making the contents of her stomach try to make its way to her mouth. His skin reminded her of the dead fish that had washed up to the river shore. She forced herself to slowly drag in a deep, steading breath. His eyes were black as onyx, except for a glow of amber where his pupil should have been, and his dark hair fell over them like a greasy curtain.

"Back it up, creeper. She's not your prize, darling." The woman glared at him until he retreated to the corner with his disgusting friend Luis. "Now Abby, my *dear* Abby, we haven't been formally introduced. My name is Marta. And you...are now mine." She winked and tapped Abby on the nose. "I'll admit that we aren't completely sure of your use, lovely, but I'd like to have you in my treasure chest just the same. Just in case, you know?"

"There's a strange business of the people that live in the shadows, isn't there baby?" Luis creeped up against the bombshell and slid his arm around her.

"Calm down, blood boy. Just because we're in business doesn't make this a deal."

Michael sidled up to her, his eyes never leaving Abby. "You've helped us track her, and you will get from her whatever it is you can get from her, but for now I think we could have more fun with her than you can."

Marta pushed Luis' arm from her and dusted off a rusty folding chair. She sat delicately and sneered at them. "No matter what you think you'll get, and no matter how you think she's yours, we all know my *boss* will tell you to back the hell off." She crossed her legs, with an eyebrow to the sky and set her eyes on the angry girl hiding her pain. "Abby, you are a sweet treat of something, aren't you? And my disgusting friends here have had their eye on you for a few months now. That makes you a bit of a treasure, doesn't it?"

"Our treasure, Marta. *Ours*." Michael's voice crawled from the corner, licking along his lips again.

Abby almost gagged looking at him and the thought of him putting one of his foul teeth right through that slimy tongue consumed her.

Michael screamed out a howl when blood started pouring down his chin. He raised his hands to his mouth, the blood not stopping.

Marta stilled in her seat staring at him. "Did you just bite your damned tongue, moron?"

Abby's heart seemed to stop watching the scene. She thought there was no way she made that happen, but she had thought it just as it happened. Michael rubbed at his face as the blood gushed, clamping his fangs down over and over again on his tongue. She willed him to keep doing it and he did.

"Michael what the hell is wrong with you? Get your shit together!" Marta rose from the chair, backing away from him.

The pain was starting to make her consciousness slip, but she knew she had to get out of there, and fast. If they were to turn on each other, it was the best chance to get away, if only she could pull her arms from the ropes. As soon as she passed the thought, Michael leapt at Luis, gnawing at his throat. Abby turned her face away from the grotesque attack but Luis' screams ripped through her mind. Squeezing her eyes as tight as she could, she just wanted it to stop. The screaming stopped after the room seemed to explode around her. The door slammed into pieces on the floor and she felt a cold splash against her face. Opening her eyes, everything was a blur of red in front of her as the small space erupted in motion.

Marta's hands were on the rope, shushing Abby soothingly. "It's ok, honey. It's over. You're ok."

Her eyes became steadier when she took deep breaths against the pain throbbing in her head; the pain in her arms sharply turned into a manageable burn as her body crumpled to the floor. She rolled her shoulders in relief and looked up into Kieran's panicked face.

"Are you ok?" His eyes searched her over desperately trying to find any sign of injury. "Where are you bleeding? Where is she fucking bleeding, Marta?" His voice boomed at her in the small room and Erick appeared behind him, holding his arms to keep him from lunging when he moved towards Marta, now pressed against the wall, terrified.

"It's not her blood, I swear, it's Michael's, not hers! I swear!"

He pulled his arms from Erick's and kneeled beside Abby, wiping gently at her face. His eyes settled on hers when he seemed to be satisfied that she was in one piece. She looked around the room, now soaked in blood. Luis was crumpled on the floor; his head angled in a way that she knew meant it wasn't completely attached anymore. When she saw Michael's body beside him, there was not question that he was dead because his head was in the corner opposite at Marta's stilettoed feet. Abby felt herself start to shake and wrapped her arms around Kieran just to feel something steady. "Abby I'm so sorry. I never should have let you go home." He deflated beside her, his arms tightening around her quaking shoulders.

Erick smoothed down his sweater and then his hair, taking in a deep breath. His mouth tried to form words that wouldn't come out before he turned to her Grandmother who was now standing in the doorway.

Gretchen surveyed the room, her eyes narrowing on Abby, before turning to Marta. "Is this your work, dear?"

Marta looked at the disfigured bodies on the floor and down at Michael's head. "No ma'am, this wasn't me. I was keeping everything calm and not letting them near her, just as you asked, but..." she trailed her eyes slowly to Abby, "they just...they just turned on each other. She...her eyes."

Erick finally found his voice. "What about her eyes?"

"She did this. She made them do this." Marta couldn't look away from Abby.

"Me?"

"Her?"

Kieran and Abby spoke in unison.

"You could see it in her eyes. She had control of them."

Kieran helped Abby to her feet, carefully supporting her weight. "What do you mean she controlled them?"

"Just that. She made them turn on each other. Her eyes locked on them and blazed the greenest I've ever seen and they...they just turned on each other." There was amazement in her voice and she started to laugh. "It was incredible! She's incredible!"

Gretchen took Abby's hands and looked her over. "Is this true, Abigail?"

"I...it can't be. I mean, I *did* want them to turn on each other. But my eyes were closed. They were closed the whole time. I didn't see anything." She looked over at Michael's face covered in blood, remembering how she wanted his to bite his sleazy tongue off and the blood that was pouring from his mouth.

"Darlin' your eyes were wide open and focused. I saw it with my own eyes. It's true! Luis' head was almost hanging from his neck and he ripped Michael's..."

Marta's words were cut off by Abby's stomach finally breaking through and she fell to her knees heaving. Kieran held her hair and rubbed her back. "That's enough Marta, she's been through enough. Erick we need to get her home."

"No, my aunt can't see me like this. Please they can't see me like this." A chill started in her chest spread to her fingers and toes.

"No Abby, you're coming home with us. There's no way you can go home right now. We need to get you home and safe. Now." Her Grandfather motioned to the door and pointed at Kieran. "Now. Put her in the car, she needs to leave now."

Kieran helped her to her feet, tucking her under his arms. "Should we wait for..."

"No, Kieran. Now!" Erick's tone turned Kieran on his heel and he shuffled Abby out. She saw her grandfather pull out his cell phone and pull Gretchen to his chest as she passed by.

The sun was rising over the dusty farm field beside them. She sat numbly in the passenger seat, not even feeling Kieran buckle her in. The ride to the manor felt like only seconds before Kieran was unbuckling her and helping her inside, her legs barely supporting her up the two flights of stairs to her room. The adrenaline had drained from her and she was tired like she had never been before. The pain ripped up and down her back, her neck throbbing and all she wanted was to crawl into a hot bath. She staggered into the bathroom and turned the water on.

"Abby you should..." Kieran helped her sit on the bench beside the tub. "You might want to take a shower first. To...rinse off."

Looking up at the long mirror above the counter she saw the mess she had become. Her face, hair and shirt were doused with blood; her eyes were dazed, lifeless.

"Ok." She stood up and started to walk into the shower like a zombie, pulling her top over her head.

"I'm gonna go get Phoebe to help you." Kieran's eyes were cast to the floor.

"No!" The mention of her friend's name brought back all the rage from the day before. "I can't deal with her right now."

"I don't want you to be alone right now, Abby." His eyes were flickering from the floor to her.

"I'm not. You're here. I don't give a shit about modesty right now, Kieran." She hung a towel on the hook outside of the tiled shower and walked around the corner; peeling off the rest of her filthy clothes and tossing them out the door, she switched on the water as hot as it would go and stood underneath. The heat streamed down her back, soothing the aching muscles that had started to tense up her neck. When she saw a bottle of shampoo on the shelf she poured a handful over her hair, scrubbing at her hair and face with it until the red water ran clear again. Michael's sneering face flashed every time she closed her eyes, his dead black eyes boring into her mind and she tried to wash away everything under the steaming showerhead. No matter how scorched her skin turned from the water, the chill running up and down her wouldn't rinse away. Closing her eyes, she leaned her head against wall, the water rolling over her sore shoulders until a settled numbness filled her body and mind. She pulled the towel from the hook, wrapped herself up and stepped out into the steam filled bathroom. Kieran was nowhere in sight but her robe was on the bench where he was sitting. She tugged it around herself and went to crawl into bed, too exhausted to wait for the bath to fill. Her head sunk into the pillow when she curled up on her side but she couldn't feel comfortable. She wanted her bed, not this prison of a room. She pulled her legs up to her chest, the tears taking her over again. This can't be her life now. This all has to be a nightmare that she'll wake up from at any moment.

"Abby?"

She looked to the door to see Phoebe poke her head through. "Fantastic, the nightmare continues."

"Can I come in? Kieran told me you were here." Abby was too tired to fight with her right now, but she needed her best friend.

"Ya, come on in." She wiped her eyes and sat up. Phoebe came through the door and held up her arms. Abby's quilt was slung over one, with a bottle of whiskey in one hand and two glasses in the other.

"My quilt! How did you get it?" Abby wrapped herself in it when she brought it over, breathing in the smell of home and sunshine.

"Kieran sent someone for it. I told him how much it means to you." She poured them each a drink and handed one to Abby.

"Thank you. I was…" her tears started again. "I was going out to get it when…" She couldn't finish her sentence, picturing the terrifying face of Michael again, feeling his cold hand around her throat. "I can't take all of this, Phoebe. This has just been a few days! I've almost been murdered by undead monsters, I have a brand new family that I've never heard about until now – and they're trying to keep me from the only family I *have* known – and I find out that my best friend in the world's father is responsible for my dad being dead! This is too screwed up for me. Can't they do the mind control trick they used on Thomas and Julie and make me forget all of this? Seriously! I can't deal with this." She took a sip from the glass, the burn of the liquor singeing her throat.

"I'm just so glad you're ok, Abbs." Phoebe reached for her hand, tears flooding her eyes.

"I'm not ok! Don't you get it? I'm not. I'm not ok with any of this!" She pulled her hand away, slamming the glass on the nightstand after draining it. "I'm not and I can't. I've had enough."

"Abby I know this is all insane but I'm here for you, I want…"

Abby's face flared with anger as she cut her off. "You want what? What, Phoebe? What do all of you want from me? Your dad killed my dad and you said nothing. Nothing! You pretended to be my friend all this time for what? Just so you could keep tabs on me for this fucked up family"

"It's nothing like that and I know you know that." They stared at each other, both too overcome with anger to find the right words.

"Why didn't you tell me, Phoebe?" Her voice was calmer, but only from fatigue.

"Why didn't I tell you my dad was a piece of shit? Why didn't I tell you, the only friend I have in the world, that my dad was insane and the reason your dad is dead?" She tried to still herself but the tears were unable to stay in her sad eyes any longer. She took a big breath and looked to the ceiling. "I'll tell you everything if you want to know, but after all that's happened…"

"After all that's happened I deserve some fucking answers!" Abby grabbed the bottle from beside her on the bed, slopping some in her glass.

"Ok. You're right." She crawled up to sit beside Abby. "But I didn't keep anything from you to hurt you. I lost my dad because of this too."

Abby sipped her glass, pondering that fact. She was completely overwhelmed but Phoebe didn't deserve her anger. "I'm sorry, I shouldn't be screaming at you but it feels like I have zero control on anything anymore. Even what I believed my whole life to be." She reached over for a tissue from the nightstand and handed the box to Phoebe. "You've been here for me for all of this, even when I didn't know you were."

"You have every right to be mad." She wiped away at her tears. "I've been mad for a long time, but know that I wasn't keeping tabs on you." She sighed, looking to Abby. "After it all happened, they just wanted to have someone with you, someone that could connect you with your family. Your mom's family, I mean. The world that she came from; and there was no way in hell I wanted to stay here after I saw…" Her voice drifted off into a memory that pained her eyes.

Abby froze at what she said before she could reach out to take her now silent friend's hand. "Oh my god, Phoebe. Did you see him do it?" Picturing her as a tiny wide-eyed little girl seeing something so horrible crushed her heart.

"I didn't see it, not like that, but..." She wouldn't look at Abby, her downcast eyes locked in thought.

All the anger Abby had erupting from her was quickly drowned in concern. She squeezed her hand, trying to coax her to go on. "Whatever it is, you can tell me."

She looked up at her with bleak eyes. "Your dad was the first death to come to me. The first vision...before it happened." The tears flowed down her face in silence again as she searched Abby's face for understanding.

"You mean...like, Banshee seeing?"

Phoebe croaked a laugh. "Ya, buttercup, like Banshee seeing. I didn't know what it was, I was really young for it to happen and when I told my mom and that my dad was..." She gulped down the whiskey and turned the glass over in her hands. "They didn't believe me, because I was so young and no one knew about..." She set her glass on the floor and turned so they were face to face. "Abby, my dad was in love with your mom." Taking both of her hands in hers, the pain in her voice wasn't as loud as the anger on her face. "He was sure they were destined to be together and when she left to be with your dad he..." Standing from the bed she grabbed the bottle of whiskey, topping each glass. "He was nuts, Abby. Grade A, certifiably, nuts ass crazy. He was married and had me. But he still killed your dad thinking that it would bring her back to them. To him. But it killed her. When your dad died it literally killed her."

"How did he give her cancer? That's not possible." Abby's heart was pounding against her ribs, shaking her to her fingertips.

"He didn't, Abbs. Somehow your mother linked with your dad. No one understands it even now, but after he died she just...faded away." She put her fingers up to her lips as if to stop herself from saying anymore and then sealed the words off with a swig of her glass. "He killed himself after that. My dad. He lost the last of his mind and killed himself. And I never told you, not only because I was sworn to secrecy, but I didn't see what good it would do for you to know."

Abby slid over on the bed and pulled Phoebe to her. "I'm so sorry. I'm so sorry for all of this. Everything that touches my mom and I gets ruined. We're some kind of freak mistake that's good only for hurting people."

Phoebe pulled away from her, fury storming in her face. "Don't you dare say that! It has nothing to do with you! You are the most wonderful, loving person I have ever known. None of this is your doing - or your mothers. My dad was messed up. He's the reason for all of this - not you and not your mom. Your mom barely even knew him."

Abby believed that Phoebe meant that; but there was a part of her that had already decided, at some point during the last few days, that she was cursed. But right now she was exhausted and glad to have her best friend with her, no matter what either of them had to do with the mess she found herself in. She sipped at her drink and started to laugh when she looked at the clock - almost noon.

"Not even lunchtime and we're on our third whiskey? What the hell has happened to us?" The tension in the room was chased away by their laughter. "I guess after being kidnapped by insane dead guys I deserve a hard liquor breakfast." They clinked glasses when Phoebe held hers up.

"I figured you could use a little something after..." She squished her face up and shrugged her shoulders. There was clearly no other words left to sum up her week, but her expression cracked the girls up again. "You're ok though, right? They didn't...hurt you?"

"No they didn't hurt me, not really. I mean, my arms and back are sore from them tying me up but they didn't touch me otherwise." Abby set her glass on the table and went into the closet to dig out some pajamas. Noon or not she was going to bed and crawled back under the heavy blankets, propping herself up with the pillows. The whiskey had warmed her up and now it was making her sleepy.

Phoebe sat down beside her and pulled the blankets up further when she yawned. "We were so scared. They wouldn't tell me anything."

"How did they find me anyways? How did they even know anything had happened to me?" Her lids started to feel heavy, the warmth of the blankets melting her into the bed. She had been trying not to think about what had happened; afraid that if she let herself remember the details that she would never come back the same. The only thing she would allow herself to focus on was when Kieran's face appeared in front of her. That was the moment that she knew she would be all right.

"I don't know, I didn't find out about it until after they had gone. I came home to chaos here."

The door creaked open and Kieran knocked lightly when he poked his head in. "How are you guys doing?" He looked from Abby to the bottle of whiskey with an amused smile, shaking his head. "I see Doctor Abby is prescribing today."

"Never question my methods, boy. I am the queen of drama-tending and you know it." She stuck out her tongue at him and stood up from Abby. "I'll leave her in your care now. I have a feeling my mother is going to want to talk to me." She kissed the top of Abby's sleepy head before turning for the door - where she hip-checked Kieran out of the way. "Take care of my girl, lover boy."

"Charmed as usual, Phoebs. Your mom is in the den with Gretchen."

She winked back at Abby when she was shutting the door. Kieran smiled back at her as he walked to Abby, sitting lightly on the bed beside her. His stiff smile was laced with concern when he was looking her over - Abby couldn't believe how endearing she found him. Normally possessive behavior like that made her uncomfortable. Her first boyfriend tried to control her as an insecure fourteen-year-old but Kieran didn't seem to want to control her, it was truly important to him that she was okay. It made her think of what Phoebe had said about her mom. Did she really die because she lost the link to her dad? Could she really have died from a broken heart? He wasn't even a Patron. Could her bond with Kieran be as deadly? Does her pain cause him pain? She couldn't handle any kind of conversation like that after what had been slammed at her already.

"How are you feeling? Can I get you anything?" He fussed with the blankets around her, making sure she was tucked in.

"I'm ok, I'm just so tired. I feel like I haven't slept in days." She yawned again.

"I'll leave you to sleep if you want, I just wanted to check in on you." He brushed the back of his fingers against her cheek, the affection tugging at Abby. She felt better having him near her and his touched told her that she didn't want him to leave.

"I'm good, I promise, but please don't go. Can you just stay with me until I fall asleep?" The thought of being alone was unsettling to Abby and the idea of staying put a beaming grin on Kieran's face, a grin that he tried to tone down when he realized he was smiling so broadly.

"Of course I will. Can I get you anything, though?"

Abby thought for a moment, unsure if she should ask. "Could you lay down with me? Until I fall asleep?" The feeling of him beside her seemed like the most comforting thing in the world when she asked, but when he timidly moved on the bed to beside her she completed relaxed. Rolling over to tuck her head into the crook of his neck she snuggled in when his arm wrapped around her. The sun was high above the trees through the window, and a cool breeze was drifting in. A sweet contrasted the warmth radiating from Kieran.

"How did you know where I was?" She kept her gaze to the window, unsure if she wanted to know the answer but unable to not ask.

"Marta. She was supposed to help keep those pieces of shit away from you. She called me as soon as she heard he..." His voice trailed off, angry.

"Marta? The woman that was there?" She felt his head nod above hers. "She must be like Marcus then, because she's definitely not like those guys."

"Marcus? You mean Marcus - Phoebes', uh, *friend?*" He seemed to try and find a polite wording.

"Ya, Marcus the vampire." Marta was nothing like the creeps that were with her, she couldn't remember what Kieran had called them, but there was something about her that told her she wasn't an average human.

"No, Marta's not a vampire or a crusnik." He traced his fingers up and down her back, enjoying the closeness and once again baffling Abby with how casual such a conversation could be for him. "She's something pretty rare nowadays, actually."

Abby chuckled to herself at that. "Really? Rarer than Vampires and Banshees and beings I've never even heard of?"

"Oh, I'm sure you've heard of her. She's a Succubus."

"What? You're kidding me." Leaning up on her elbow, she had to see his face - he had to be joking. He was smiling down at her, eyes sparkling with amusement at her reaction, but she could tell he wasn't teasing her. "Seriously?"

"I am serious, yes." His lighthearted chuckle made her warm. "She comes from, shall we say, a darker side of our people but she is very loyal to your family. She had heard rumblings of the notice you had received by those…savages, and wanted to help."

Suddenly the contented moment passed and instead the terror she felt in the shed overcame her. She tried to stop the tears but they burned down her face, blood feeling cold again, she started to shake. Her mind filled with Michael's disgusting tongue snaking his lips, his dead eyes drinking her in and Luis' screams as they ripped each other apart. Kieran tugged her back to him; his arms tight around her he kissed her hair when she buried her face in his shirt.

"It's ok, Abby, you're ok now. I'm not going to let anything happen to you again." His jaw set tightly, not letting her go. "I should have insisted more that you stay here."

Abby squeezed her eyes closed, willing away the waking nightmare she had flashing in her mind. She forced herself to feel his arms around her, to let the smell of him envelope her, to let the cool breeze from the window tickle her face. Anything to convince herself that she was safe now. They lay in silence like that for some time, before Abby nodded off into a dreamless sleep.

Chapter 9

When she did manage to pull her eyes open again the room was dark. Looking over to clock she realized she had slept all day and her stomach agreed with her. If her eating habits carried on as they had in the last few days she would die of starvation. Kieran's arm was slung over her hip and she was surprised with how comfortable she felt with a virtual stranger laying so intimately against her, but she supposed the hurricane of emotions she'd been slammed with over that time would have to have some effect on her feelings to him.

"Are you feeling any better?"

Abby rolled over to find Kieran lying on his side, regarding her. "A little, ya. I really needed sleep." She felt sheepish suddenly, almost nose to nose with him. "Thank you for staying with me."

"Of course, it was my pleasure." A shy grin twitched at his lips. "Can I get you anything?"

"No, thank you though. I'd just like to lie here and hide from the world for a little longer, if that's ok." She rolled her neck back and forth, feeling the burn of the strained muscles in her shoulders. At some point she knew she had to find her Grandparents and ask another round of the millions of questions that had been rolling around in her head, but she didn't have the energy for any of that. Kieran locked his fingers around hers, pressing her hand to his lips.

"Whatever you want, Abby. Just let me know."

The way he looked at her, the way her heart noticed every time he looked at her like that, made her feel like the world that hers had become could be worth it as long, as she was with him. The dim light the moon cast through the window lit up his eyes, the sparkle irresistible. She leaned closer until her lips brushed his lightly, wanting to get lost in him and just forget about everything. His kiss was soft at first, trying to be gentle with her sore body but she wasn't having that. Her kiss deepened when he let go of her hand to trace his fingers up her leg, to her hip, rolling her back onto the bed. His lips were soft and warm, her body responding to every inch of his body touching hers. The heat spread through her body while his hands roamed her, and a soft moan slipped from her.

"Are you getting up yet- oh my god! Shit! Sorry!" Phoebe's voice rang through the room before the door slammed.

Kieran didn't move from above Abby but he made a pained smile when he looked down at her. Abby's hand went up to her face, laughing at Phoebe's reaction when he kissed her quickly on her nose and rolled over to the side lamp to switch it on. He lay on his side again, smiling when Abby turned to him.

"I'm guessing you two have sorted some things out?"

"We did, yes." She rubbed her hands over her face to shake her hormones out of her head, the moment seemingly passed. "I feel bad for being so angry and shouting at her."

"I'd never heard of any of that until yesterday when you overheard... well, anyways, it certainly explains why Gretchen has been so cold towards Phoebe for as long as I remember."

"I feel so bad. She's had this weight on her for so long and it has nothing to do with her." Abby stood beside the bed to switch on the other lamp and then stretched her sore arms above her, everything feeling tight.

"I can't imagine it was easy for her. But, everyone carries the sins of their family, I suppose. And if you stand as a family, you have to stand for each member. You have to take responsibility for their actions and so every action we make, our families make. We can't just walk away if we want to keep our families strong. Phoebe certainly has had the burden of her dad's actions on her for a long time. She's a pretty strong girl to carry all of that in secret. I suppose that's why you two are so close. You both are woman much stronger than anyone could imagine."

Abby had never thought of herself as a strong woman but she was quite proud of herself for how she's handled the insanity that had been slammed in front of her – minus the break down on Phoebe today. But Aunt Julie always told her she needed to take a day to fall apart. That she held in too much all the time and she should take a day to just fall apart. Let all the pieces fall where they may, and step back to get a better look at the puzzle. Just so long as you made sure you got back to work on that puzzle when you're done. And that's just what she was going to have to do now, no matter how impossible that seemed. She would just have to find away to balance everything now with what she had always known. She couldn't live without the family that had raised her just because the new one believed it would be easier for her to just abandon them.

"Are my Aunt and Uncle ok? They didn't go near them did they?" She felt horrible that this was the first time that she had thought of them since she was attacked.

"They're fine. They didn't hear a thing and no one went near them. Don't worry, I promise. But..." He sat up on the bed, running a hand through his hair. "It's not going to be safe for you to live there anymore, you understand that now don't you?" He was right and she knew it, but it still crushed her. She couldn't live with herself if whatever she was hurt them. But she couldn't – and wouldn't – live without them. "Abby? Do you know what happened? With Michael?"

Her eyes fixed on him, concerned. "What do you mean do I know? Do I know that they kidnapped me and tied me up to be dinner?" She hoped that's all that had happened. If something else had happened and she didn't remember it, she wanted it to stay that way.

He moved over to the edge of the bed, beside where she was standing, and took her hand. "No, I mean do you remember what you did?" He looked up at her, looking unsure of his question.

"What I did? What did I do?"

"When we got there, they were...dead. Did you know that?"

Did she know that? Of course she knew that, she could still hear the screams of them turning on each other, ripping each other to pieces. She crossed her arms, trying to understand what he meant with the question. "I knew they were fighting but I kept my eyes closed. I didn't see they were dead until you were there."

He stood up beside her and kissed her forehead. "I think you should go have a nice long bath and then come downstairs for something to eat. You must be starving." He tilted his head down so they were eye to eye, pressing a soft kiss to her lips. "Meet me in the kitchen, ok?" He gently squeezed her hand before he turned for the door.

A bath was exactly what she needed, the hot water relaxing her shoulders. It was the first chance she had to actually see the damage those monsters had done to her. The deep purple bruises were striped with raw welts from where she pulled at the ropes. A slash of red scratches across her breast burned when the water covered it and she was glad she couldn't remember how she got them. She took long, deep breaths when the fear started to bubble its way up to her chest again, turning her focus back to the soothing water. Her mother had taught her to calm herself that way when she was very little and her emotions seemed so strong that she had no control of her body, filled with tantrums. The slow deep breaths, eyes focused on something calming, settled her in a way that nothing else could. It was one of the reasons why she seemed to be so reserved, why Julie always wanted her to pitch a fit, instead of bottling things up, but she felt more in control when kept a lock on her emotions. The tops of the trees were dancing in the early summer breeze, lit up by the clear night sky, and she stared out the window focusing on her breathing until her hunger pulled her downstairs. She threw on some sweats, grimacing at the cuffs rubbing her wrists, and went down to the kitchen. Kieran smiled up at her from the stove and Phoebe was perched on one of the stools across from him.

"I was just apologizing for interrupting you earlier." Phoebe giggled, cracking open a soda and handing it her. "Are you feeling any better?"

Abby smelled the familiar scent of mac and cheese drift over to her, and smiled when she realized Kieran was stirring a big pot of it. "I will be when I eat that." She sat beside Phoebe at the counter as Marcus strolled in, popping onto the seat on the other side of her friend.

"I never did get to try that. I think I may have liked it." He sharp white teeth shone in a friendly grin. "So, my scrumptious little treat, how is the delicate little mortal that has stolen you from my bed?" He leaned into Phoebe, a cocky eyebrow pushed up above playful eyes.

"Shut up, Marcus. Mind your manners." She laughed but a flush grew across her pale cheek. "I never meant to break your cold little heart. But my love life is none of your business."

"Love life? The fabulous Miss Phoebe has a love life?" Abby turned her stool to face her. "Could this have something to do with a certain bartender?"

"Everyone just mind their own business. I have nothing to share." Phoebe and Kieran shared a look that Abby couldn't understand but Kieran did not look pleased. "Marcus if you're only here to make trouble for me, you can leave now."

Kieran set filled bowls in front of each of the girls. "He's here at Gretchen's request, Phoebe. And he'd be best to go find her now, don't you think Marcus?" The unsettling look he had given to Phoebe the first night in the pub was now set on the smiling vampire.

"My, my. This house has become so tense lately. You all need to have some fun!" He leaned down close to Phoebes' ear. "I'm still available for fun whenever you need me, doll." He made a kissy face at her when she elbowed him away. He was still laughing to himself when he left the kitchen.

They ate in uncomfortable silence for a few minutes. Abby couldn't talk if she wanted to with the way she was cramming the hot cheesy noodles in her mouth, forkful after forkful. Her appetite had apparently met its breaking point. Her bowl was empty before it had a chance to cool down.

"I told you she'd make it disappear in under five minutes." Phoebe smiled over her own forkful. "Kieran said he was worried that you hadn't eaten much lately. I betrayed you and gave up your secret weakness. Forgive me?"

Abby smiled at them. "I can forgive anything for mac and cheese."

"She's not lying. A single box got me forgiveness for borrowing her favorite sweater without asking. And I returned it ripped! Didn't even need to make the damn box, just handed it over."

"You forgot to include that it was ripped because you were making out with Bobby McMann up against a pine tree."

They all laughed when Phoebe shrugged her shoulders with a crooked smile. "What can I say, he liked that sweater."

Abby was so happy to have such a normal moment, it made it seem as if life here could be livable - if she had no choice but to stay. Kieran brushed a kiss on her neck when he came around to scoop up her bowl to toss in the soapy sink. They chatted as if the last days had been nothing more than a fading nightmare. But she knew it wouldn't last and it didn't.

Maggie appeared at the doorway. "So sorry to interrupt, but Mr. and Mrs. Ambrose are ready for you both." She nodded a smile before turning back through the door.

"Well that's my cue. I'm gonna go make sure Marcus hasn't set up camp in my bed. I'll talk to you in a bit, ok?" Phoebe gave her a rub on her back as she passed by.

"Can't you come with us? I feel so much better when you're with me." Abby grabbed her hand.

"Sorry, buttercup, but this sounds like business. And business that isn't mine." She gave her a sympathetic smile. "I'll be just upstairs and Kieran will be with you. Don't worry, things will level out soon. I promise."

They followed her out of the kitchen to go into the den. She smiled again, encouragingly, at Abby when she started up the stairs. Kieran took Abby's hand and walked to the den, knocking lightly on the door before opening it. Her grandparents were sitting on one of the sofas, with Marcus and Marta on the other. Thomas stood when he saw her, and approached her cautiously.

"My dear girl, how are you feeling?" His hands twitched up, unsure if he should attempt to hug her, deciding instead to gesture for them to sit.

She sat beside her grandmother who grasped her hand sweetly. "I'm feeling better, considering."

Her grandfather sat gingerly beside her when Kieran sat opposite.

"I'm well aware of how much has happened to you and I would like nothing more than to give you some time to make peace with this all, but as you are now well aware, you are in danger."

Gretchen kept Abby's hand in hers as she spoke. "We had always assumed that there could be certain things about you that are unique in a way that would set you apart from us. Certain things that could make you appealing to individuals that are not looking out for your best intentions."

Abby turned her confused eyes to Kieran who, despite giving her a friendly smile, looked tense. Even Marcus, beside him, seemed serious. She turned back to her Grandmother. "What am I supposed to do about it?"

Thomas took her other hand. "It's not so much what you can do about it, as what we believe you have already done." She looked back and forth between the somber faces set on her. "Abigail, do you have a clear recollection of what happened last night?"

"I, um, was taken by Michael and tied up in a shed." She was trying to think of anything she could have done that would put her in further danger than being kidnapped from her backyard just because of who her mother was.

"That's right. And do you remember Marta being there? In the shed with you?" Thomas spoke gently to her. Abby looked up at Marta, whose plump lips were turned up in a small smile.

"Yes of course I remember her. And I remember the other creep and I remember you guys coming in. I remember all of it. Why are you asking me this?" She pulled her hands from her grandparents and crossed her arms protectively across her chest.

"Do you remember why the crusniks attacked each other?" Gretchen kept her voice soft and even.

"No my eyes were closed. I was terrified. Ask *her* if you want the details. She was the one who wasn't tied up and told she was dinner." She didn't mean to sound so cold, but she'd had enough of the question and answer portion of this conversation. "Can someone tell me what's going on?"

Marta leaned forward from the sofa. "If I may?" Gretchen nodded to her. "Sweetie, first off, I am so very sorry for how we met. I tried my best to keep them away from you, but they are truly a deviant bunch." Abby just stared at her, no idea what to say to a Succubus who just called her sweetie. "I'm a very old woman, if you were to go by the years you would see in a lifetime. I'm even ancient compared to this guy who's been sucking on blood for more than two centuries." Marcus stifled a chuckle at his mention. "But being so old has given me knowledge of some of the things that have become lost as generations of mortals turn over. And that's what this is about, darling."

Abby leaned forward to her. "Then please tell me. I don't think there's anything left that can shock me."

"I've known women like you and your mother before you. To the Patrons now, you're folklore. Nothing more than a story, because there have been so few of you. But I know different, as do they now. You, darling, are touched with energies that none of us have. Whatever spark the universe uses, when it decides that the world is ready for another one like you, it's strong. And there are beings out there that want to take advantage of that power, even though they don't know what it is or how it works, they want it."

"Powers like what? I don't have any powers." Abby was more confused than before Marta had attempted to explain. She didn't have x-ray vision or super-strength or anything above average about her.

"Sweetheart, I saw it in your eyes. It's something I've seen before and not something I could ever forget. The fire in your eyes right before it happened. I know that fire."

Abby rubbed her forehead, trying to understand. "What fire? Fire before what?"

Gretchen took her hand again. "Abigail, do you remember what you were thinking when they attacked each other?"

Abby pictured the face she'd been trying to forget - Michael and his stench in front of her. "I...I wanted him to bite his disgusting tongue off."

Her grandmother's hand tightened on hers. "And then?"

She pictured the blood pouring out of his mouth, the three of them shouting around her. "I just wanted to find a way out and they were fighting. I wanted them to turn on each...Wait. Are you trying to say I *made* them do those things?" There's no way she had mind control over those creatures. She had the thought pass her mind at the time but she knew it was impossible.

"You wouldn't be the first of your kind to have that ability. It's rare, even considering how rare you are to begin with, darling. But it's possible. I saw you. I saw your eyes, I saw what they did to each other."

"No, no, no, no, no. I didn't do that. I couldn't have. They were insane! They did it themselves."

Thomas put his arm around her shoulder tenderly. "My dear, they weren't the first to try to steal you from us. There are those that live a darker life and will do anything to gain power. If this is true, if you have these abilities, more will come for you."

Abby held her hands up, trying to process the newest conversation to melt her brain. "Come for me for what? I don't have any super powers, you're all crazy."

"Your Grandparents are very powerful people. They have a lot of power over a lot of people. And some of those people resent that. Supernaturally natured people are just like those you were raised with in a sense of some are good and some are bad. Do you know what I mean?" Abby nodded her head slightly to her. "Now if you were to be able to control them with whatever gift you may have, and if they could find a way to control you…"

"They could control the others." Abby pictured a world where Michael and Luis had the power over monsters in the same way her grandparents did.

"That's right. And if they controlled you, they could turn others against the Patrons. They have had immense power for a reason, for a very long time. If they were to be removed from power, it would be chaos." Marta leaned back into the couch, crossing her long legs. "You're a pretty little weapon that we need to understand."

"What she means to say is that you could possibly have something inside you that could effectively change how we rule. We need to keep you safe until we understand what all of this means. My dear, you seem to become more extraordinary by the day." Gretchen regarded her with pride.

"She must take after you, Ambrose." Marcus winked at Erick.

"Don't suck up, son. It's off putting." Erick turned his attention back to Abby. "We never wanted this sort of responsibility to be put on you, but if it's true there isn't very much we can do except keep you safe. And I promise you, we will."

"How can we even know if I have any super powers?"

Marcus chuckled again and was given an elbow to the ribs by Kieran.

"Well that's why we have our guests here. Marta has been sharing with us what all of this could all mean. If it's true, we can go from there and make educated choices on how to keep you, and all of us really, safer."

"Patrons such as yourself have the ability to control other-natured's. Marcus here is our test subject." Marta patted him on the leg and he grinned at them all. "Like I said, he's much younger than I am and was once a transient so if it's true you should be able to have an effect on him. If *that's* true, we can try your effect on me, but with my age and how I'm natured, it mostly likely won't affect me. It doesn't hurt to try though."

"So, what? I just tell him to do something and he'll do it?" Abby felt ridiculous even saying it.

"Give it a try. See what happens." Kieran smiled at her hoping to encourage her.

"Ok. How can this be any stranger than the rest of this, right?" She sat up straight between her grandparents and locked her eyes on Marcus'. "Bark like a dog."

The room was silent as everyone looked back and forth between the two of them.

Marcus' eyebrows shot up when his lips pursed into an uncomfortable grin. "Uh, nope. Nothing. Sorry."

Kieran sat forward, leaning towards Abby. "It's ok. Try again, try to focus on what you're saying."

Abby shook her head, frustration building in her. "This is stupid." She looked to Marcus again. "Bark like a dog. Bark, Marcus!" Marcus bit his lip trying to hold in a laugh, making her frustration start to become anger. He took a sip from a wine glass. "Ok, then. Give me your wine, Marcus."

"Oh, that's awkward, love. This is definitely not wine." He started to full on laugh as he took a big gulp of the deep red liquid.

"Oh my god, that's disgusting. I don't want to deal with any of this right now. I need some air." She started to get up from the couch when Kieran rose to stop her.

"Please, Abby, we're not trying to frustrate you. We want to help, but you need to *let us* help you." He reached his hands for hers, his eyes pleading. She pulled her hands away from him and stepped back.

"I can't deal with all of this right now. You're obviously wrong about me. I have no power over him at all. This is silly."

"I wouldn't say no power over me, beautiful. I could think of a few things you could control on me." Marcus gave her a sultry gaze and a lusty fanged grin.

"Marcus shut your bloody mouth or I'll shut it for you." Kieran's rage was rolling off of him when he tried to take her hands again. Abby felt like she couldn't breathe, her heart beating harder and the emotions in room making it feel like it was closing in around her.

"Enough! Enough of all of this."

"You heard the doll. Ease up Kieran."

The mocking in his voice put her over the edge. She slammed herself back on the couch, her head in her hands and screamed at them. "You both need to fuck off and leave me alone!"

She didn't mean to be so harsh but Marcus' flippant attitude and Kieran's possessiveness was too much to deal with at the moment. She looked up to apologize but found them both walking out the door.

"Kieran! Marcus! Get back in here this instant!" Thomas' voice boomed as he followed behind them, but they ignored him and walked out the door, shutting it quietly behind them. Abby wiped at tears she hadn't realized were forming and looked to her shocked grandmother, her hand tightly around her pearls. Thomas opened the door and followed the boys out with a flourish of obscenities, demanding they return.

"Did she…Did she just…" Gretchen's voice was barely more than a whisper.

"Not only did she, she did it to a Patron as well." Marta stared at Abby like she had just levitated in front of her, a mix of awe and fear in her eyes. "Well fuck me. That's a first."

## Chapter 10

The room was silent when Abby looked back and forth between the two women. They stared at her, shock locked on both of their faces.

"Oh come on, I didn't do that." If she had any power over them, it was the power of tantrum. She refused to believe that she made them leave.

"Did you see her eyes before she sat down?" Marta spoke to Gretchen but her eyes didn't leave Abby, the look of shock turning to fear.

"I do believe I did." Gretchen put her hand on Abby's knee. "My dear, this is bigger than we could have ever imagined."

Abby felt her eyes roll in disbelief. She was able to believe a lot of what they had told her, especially the things they had *shown* her, but she would have to feel something if she had the ability to control people. She was sure of that. They were just reading into everything now and she didn't want any part of it.

"Abby, you're something else! Girl, you'd scare an A-bomb!" Abby gave Marta a frustrated glare.

"Marta, your presence is no longer required here. And I don't believe I have to specify the result of you speaking with anyone in regards to what has transpired here." Gretchen's voice was suddenly cold.

"No ma'am you do not. I'll show myself out." She scurried to the door and disappeared in a flash.

"You can't honestly believe that I did that." Abby watched her grandmother rise from the couch and walk over to the window, her hands twisted in her pearls again. "Seriously. I pitched a fit and they left. They just left, that's all. I can't control minds."

"Abigail, I wish that were true. I have hated the pressure that has been put on you simply from us being revealed to you, but this is a weight on your shoulders that pains me." She turned back to her. "But it will be alright. I swear to you, Abigail, we will keep you safe. We'll find a way to understand this."

Abby cringed at how serious Gretchen's voice was. This couldn't be true. She went from recent college grad to queen of the freaks in a matter of days. "Wouldn't it be best if you just did that mind trick thing and made me forget about all of this. Can't we just go back to how it was?" Abby was surprised that she wasn't crying, it was as if she had run out of tears over the last few days. She had gone through more emotions in the last few days than she did when she lost her parents. She was drained.

Gretchen crossed over to her quickly and pulled her into a soft embrace. "It's not that easy my dear. This isn't something you can forget, and even if you were to forget it wouldn't change who you are. You would be in even more danger and I will not let anything further harm you. And I believe it's not something that would work for you anyways. You're still half Patron." She pulled her tighter when the door opened. Erick slipped in, with a dazed looking Kieran behind him. Abby jumped up from Gretchen's arm and ran to him, throwing her arms around him.

"Tell them, Kieran. Tell them I didn't make you do that!" His arms slowly moved around her waist.

"I really wish I could. But…" He looked down at her, his eyes filled with confusion and awe. "I've never felt anything like that. Ever. In my life."

"Don't say that, please, tell them you just left because I was mad." She pleaded with him, as if the words spoken would be enough to make all of it go away. He held her hand tightly and walked them over to sit. Erick sat beside Gretchen and they shared a sad glance before they turned back to Abby, who was staring at the carpet, her shoulders slumped in defeat.

"Where did Marcus go?" her voice was small now, the fight gone from her.

"He left. When I caught up to them, they were on the porch. They seemed to be getting their wits about them again and then he left." Erick rubbed at his head before sitting back. "Well, luckily, my sweet Abby, your grand pappy always has more than one plan."

Abby laughed lightly at the moniker and looked up to him. "And what would that be?"

"Well the first part pleases me greatly. You will most definitely need to remain here, in our care, for everyone's safety." Abby started to argue but he held his hand up to stop her. "Please let me finish. You will not be here against your will, and we will do everything in our power to make it as wonderful for you as we can. But, we have the means to protect you on a higher level with you at the manor and, as I have said before, I will not let anything happen to you. I will not lose you, Abby." He paused to smile at her and there was a love in his gaze that made Abby believe him. "The second thing we must do is get in touch with a gentleman by the name of Allen Salley."

"Do you really believe he can help, Erick?" Gretchen sat forward, hope washing over her face.

"I truly do, my love. Abby, he has knowledge of others that have lived long ago. Others we believe to be...as you are. And I've been told he can help you develop the power that has been discovered within you. To help you understand it, and control it."

Abby shook her head. "I still don't believe I have the power to do anything. I honestly think you're all mistaken. You're reading into something that isn't even there."

"Well, he can also confirm that for you. I must be honest with you, Abby. I don't believe we are mistaken. And even if we were to be wrong about you, enough people, with poor intentions, have become aware of you. They don't bother with facts or reality when it comes to trying to gain power. We will bring Mr. Salley here to spend some time with you, and that will give us a new direction in which to move forward. This is new territory for all of us, but it's nothing we cannot manage."

Abby wasn't happy with the idea of being something that needed to be 'managed'. "So your plan is to keep me here and have some guy assess my apparent super magic powers? Seriously? That's the conversation we're having right now? That's not much of a plan, and it certainly doesn't make my time here as wonderful as you implied it would be."

Erick chuckled. "Plans are my forte, not timing, unfortunately. There is a third part to my plan, being prepared that will make you quite happy, I'm sure. And Mr. Bernard actually deserves the credit for the idea."

Kieran, the daze now gone from his eyes, put his arm around her. "Everything is going to work out. I promise you, Abby. I know it's my fault you had to be pulled into all of this and I will spend my entire life making it up to you." It broke her heart to hear him blame himself for all of this. She didn't know who to blame anymore, but she knew she would have been whatever the hell it was that she was whether Kieran existed or not. He was the best part of all of this craziness. She put her palm to his warm cheek and he leaned into her. "I swear, Abby, things will get better."

"I want to believe that. I really do, but I feel like I'm a black cloud over your lives and if I weren't around there wouldn't be any problems."

"I know I speak for everyone, especially Kieran, when I say that's just nonsense. You are my only Granddaughter and we love you dearly. You are a piece of us and belong with us."

A knock on the door startled her, and Phoebe stuck her head in. "I think they're good to go, Mr. Ambrose." She blazed a smile at Abby and gave her a little wave.

Gretchen gave Erick a quizzical look and he simply smiled back. She took something away from his expression and clasped her hands together. "Did you? Oh Erick, thank you. It's the right choice. This is wonderful!"

Abby looked to everyone in turn, realizing she was the only one in the room that didn't know what was going on. A feeling that was getting far too familiar lately.

"Hey sunshine. Quite the digs, huh?" Her heart leapt from her chest when her Uncle's voice filled the room. She bounded from the sofa to him and her aunt who was smiling away.

"Oh my god, what are you guys doing here?" She turned to Kieran, "How are they here?"

"You need your family with you, so here they are. We had someone pay them a visit earlier to have a *talk* with them." Kieran grinned mischievously and gave her a wink.

She hugged them both to her. "You mean they don't know? About…they don't know?"

"We don't know what?" Julie was still smiling at everyone as she asked.

Gretchen came to take Julie's hands in hers. "Nothing, dear. Phoebe, why don't you take them up to their room and get them settled. We've all had a very long day."

"That sounds good. I have a touch of a headache tonight. There must be a storm coming." Julie gave Abby another squeeze. "I'll see you in the morning, pretty girl. This is so exciting!"

Thomas gave everyone a quick wave. "Ok, Phoebe, lead on. Let's get this lady to bed. I've got a date with that lake and a fishing rod tomorrow. Thanks again for having us, Gretchen, Erick." He gave a quick nod and as fast as they appeared they were gone. Abby looked back to her grandparents dumbfounded. "How?"

"It's going to take a lot of maintenance, but as I told you before, we have a way of making Transients see what we want them to see. And if you're to be happy here, I know you need them with you." Gretchen was smiling broadly at Erick. "Thank you, my love. It's the right choice."

"It would be for the best that we are able to watch over them, as well. It would be unspeakable to allow something to happen to them because of our position." Her grandfather sounded very serious when he spoke. There really was a regal authority to him.

"So do they know anything about all of this?" Abby was so happy, but equally as confused.

"No they do not. And they must not. They believe they are here for a holiday with you and your lovely old grandparents." He strode over to the wet bar.

"And what will they think when a vampire or a goblin strolls by them in the hall?" Abby didn't want to talk them out of having them here but it couldn't be that easy to just tell them everything.

"They won't see them as they appear. Don't worry, it was a top carriager that met with them and they won't suspect a thing." Kieran took her hand when she sat on the couch beside him again.

"They'll have no idea and it won't be permanent. Just a little vacation, and all the bases were covered. It's just until things get sorted out a little. You can have them here with you and we'll know you're all safe."

Abby felt a weight lift off of her that had been crushing her the last few days. Having her aunt and uncle there with her, knowing they weren't in danger of some undead creep skulking around their house, and being able to see them whenever she wanted, made everything feel more bearable. She felt a smile spread across her face and jumped with a start when Erick popped a bottle of champagne. Kieran laughed at her reaction, clearly pleased to finally see her smiling.

"I think we should toast to our new beginning as a family." Erick filled four crystal flutes and Gretchen gathered two for Abby and Kieran before they all raised them to each other. "To have you here Abby, a piece of my Lucy, fills my heart. There will be trials ahead of us, but we will face them together, as a family. We will find the joy in life again because we will have each other. Even in the rain you can dance, my dear. Cheers to you all." They sipped at their glasses and Abby sat back in disbelief. Could it really be that easy? She wasn't sure but for the first time she knew she was willing to try. Kieran's soft lips brushed her cheek and she looked up at his adoring grin. Things could certainly be worse.

Hope you enjoyed The Patrons by Katherine Dempster.
Please check out
http://www.dreambigpublishing.net/
for more info on the books in our collection.

Made in the USA
Charleston, SC
12 July 2016